Leah angled her head away, but Jaco caught hold of her chin and turned her to face him again. He was clearly going to spare her no mercy.

"Don't."

"Don't what?" With the compelling force of Jaco's glittering gaze stealing all reason, Leah had no idea about anything anymore.

"Don't think."

Jaco helpfully supplied her with the answer, tracing her jawline with a featherlight finger that rippled a slide of sensation through her senses.

"Thinking only gets you into trouble. Now is the time to *show* me how sorry you are for keeping my son a secret."

"Who says I'm sorry?"

The arrogance of this man was astounding. As was the sudden lack of air in the room, and the sweeping sexual current that was dragging her under, making it impossible to breathe.

"*I* do, Leah."

Andie Brock started inventing imaginary friends around the age of four and is still doing that today—only now the sparkly fairies have made way for spirited heroines and sexy heroes. Thankfully, she now has some real friends, as well as a husband and three children, plus a grumpy but lovable cat. Andie lives in Bristol and when not actually writing might well be plotting her next passionate romance story.

Books by Andie Brock

Harlequin Presents

The Last Heir of Monterrato
The Greek's Pleasurable Revenge
Vieri's Convenient Vows

One Night With Consequences

The Shock Cassano Baby

Wedlocked!

Bound by His Desert Diamond

Society Weddings

The Sheikh's Wedding Contract

Visit the Author Profile page
at Harlequin.com for more titles.

Andie Brock

KIDNAPPED FOR HER SECRET SON

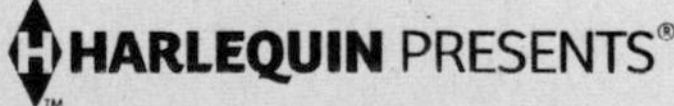

ISBN-13: 978-1-335-50476-0

Kidnapped for Her Secret Son

First North American publication 2018

This edition published by arrangement with Harlequin Books S.A.

For questions and comments about the quality of this book, please contact us at CustomerService@Harlequin.com.

Printed in U.S.A.

KIDNAPPED FOR HER SECRET SON

For Jo

PROLOGUE

'*Buonasera!*'

He was beside her in a couple of long strides. All towering height and dark, sexy masculinity, he was wearing expensively cut suit trousers and a white shirt tugged open at the throat. His black leather shoes were already sprinkled with a coating of dry Sicilian dust. Immediately his hands went to cup her face and he lowered his head to capture her mouth with a kiss full of possession and promise.

Leah leant in to him, her eyelids closing as she breathed in his familiar cologne mingled with his heat and scent after several hours' travelling. She had been longing for this moment for weeks. But now…

'Mmm, that's better.' Pulling away, Jaco let his arms drop and, finding her hands by her sides, linked his fingers through hers. 'You look…*bellissima*.' His intensely dark brown eyes raked hungrily over her body.

'Thank you.'

'I've missed you.'

'I've missed you too.' Leah focussed on keeping her voice steady. 'It's been a long time, Jaco.'

'Yes, too long.' Running his hands over her cheeks, he kissed her softly on the lips again. 'But now I am here I intend to make it up to you.'

He pulled her closer to him, the evidence of how he intended to do that already making itself felt.

Leah gently pushed him away. 'So how long are you here for?' She tilted her head to meet his.

'I should be able to manage a couple of days.' Jaco held her gaze, stroking a seductive finger along her jawline as if reacquainting himself with her face.

'Two days?' Leah rearranged her features to hide her disappointment.

'Sí.' He smiled at her—the sort of smile that could break a thousand hearts the world over. 'So we'll have to make the most of the time while we have it.'

'Yes.' She bit down on her lip. 'I suppose we will.'

'Right, I'm going to grab a shower, and maybe something quick to eat, and then I am

very much hoping we can pick up where we left off.' The wicked gleam in his eyes left no room for doubt as to where that would be.

Where they'd left off. Leah's stomach swooped at the memory of the last night they had spent together. The wonderful intimacy they had shared before Jaco had disappeared from her life yet again.

Jaco Valentino: tall, dark, ridiculously handsome, flirty, funny and sexy…knee-shakingly sexy… He was impossible to ignore or resist. Introduced to her by her twin sister, Harper, at Harper's wedding to Vieri, it had been lust at first sight for Leah. A sledgehammer kind of attraction—the sort you never really recovered from.

So when Jaco had invited her to visit his vineyard the next day she had accepted right away, any ideas about being more cautious, more circumspect, somehow blown to the wind. He had described the Capezzana estate as his 'Sicilian roots', and his obvious pride in the place had made her fall in love with it before she had even seen it. She'd known she might fall for its owner too, if she wasn't very careful.

And Capezzana had proved to be every bit as enchanting as Jaco had said. With its rows upon rows of neat vines against a stunning

backdrop of dark mountains, not to mention an imposing eighteenth-century *palazzo*, it was picture-perfect. The few days they had stayed there had been wonderful—*special*—as they had begun to get to know one another, sharing stories, chatting, laughing, sampling the delicious Capezzana wine—probably too much of it in Leah's case.

Although her light-headedness had been more likely down to the company than the alcohol. Jaco Valentino was like no man she had ever met before. Somehow he made her feel as if the ground beneath her feet was no longer quite solid, as if the sky was more intensely blue, the air suddenly in short supply. It was a dangerously exhilarating feeling, but Leah had sternly told herself to stamp it down, not to let herself get carried away.

Because Leah had learnt never to trust a man. Starting with her father, who had turned to drink when she'd needed him most, it seemed to Leah that the opposite sex had done nothing but let her down her whole life.

Okay, maybe she was partly to blame. She was impulsive by nature, and a series of bad judgements had landed her in trouble more times than she cared to remember. *Act first and think later.* The phrase might have been invented for her. And it seemed there were

plenty of men only too happy to take advantage of that.

From the job interview in Morocco, when she had ended up slapping the guy's sleazy face after she'd found out what was really involved, to stupidly losing all her money to a gambling addict in Atlantic City, she had managed to mess up all over the world.

But only once had she lost her heart, and that had been in her home town of Glenruie, in the wilds of Scotland. At the age of eighteen, finally fit and healthy after the years of kidney problems that had plagued her young life, she had fallen head over heels for a handsome young redhead called Sam, the son of the local Laird. The same Laird who owned the Craigmore estate, which employed her entire family. Leah and Harper had both worked at the lodge, and their father, Angus, was the head gamekeeper.

The whole thing had ended in misery. Several months into their relationship Leah had discovered that Sam was engaged to someone else—a titled lady, no less. And not only that, as employees at the lodge Leah and Harper had had to wait on the happy couple at their wedding.

When a bowl of cock-a-leekie soup had mysteriously ended up in the groom's lap,

Leah had been hauled before the Laird and told in no uncertain terms that if she and her sister wanted to keep their jobs—and more importantly if they wanted their father to keep his, a job he was only hanging on to by a thread anyway, because of his drinking—Leah had better change her ways.

And so she had. Simmering with the injustice of it all, while trying to hide her poor broken heart, she had vowed she was never going to be stupid enough to fall in love again.

Which was why, even though the sexual chemistry between her and Jaco had been off the scale from the start, she had done her very best to keep herself grounded, not to give in to her feelings. Concentrating instead on trying to work out exactly who this darkly handsome stranger was. To figure him out rather than let the explosion of desire knock her off her feet.

And it had seemed that Jaco felt the same way. Flirtatious and tactile from the start, he had never tried to hide his attraction to her, but at the same time he had tantalisingly held back from attempting to take it any further. Treating their relationship like an unexploded bomb, he had handled it so carefully that Leah hadn't known whether to swoon or scream.

So when the time had come for them to leave—Jaco to fly back to New York, and Leah reluctantly to return to her family home—she had told herself that that was that. With no mention of their meeting up again, she had swallowed her disappointment and pasted on a brilliant smile, only letting it slip very slightly when Jaco had enfolded her in his strong, warm embrace to give her a tight hug.

Lord, he'd felt *so* good. Pulling back, he had looked into her eyes for a long, mesmerising moment, before turning to stride away, taking a regretful little piece of Leah's heart with him.

However, twelve months later they had met again. On discovering they were both to be godparents to Harper and Vieri's baby son, Leah hadn't been able to stop the rush of excitement. And when, a week before the christening, she'd received Jaco's text message, saying how much he was looking forward to seeing her again, her whole body had started to sing and dance in anticipation.

But she'd known she *had* to be sensible. That text had been the only contact she'd had with him in a whole year. She had no idea what he'd been up to, who he had been seeing. He might well have a girlfriend by now—a

whole string of girlfriends for all she knew. He looked as if he could handle it.

Trying to grill Harper for information about him had proved frustratingly unproductive. Even though he was Vieri's oldest friend, it seemed Jaco Valentino played his cards very close to his chest. Slowly it had begun to dawn on Leah that she actually knew very little about this man who had had such a powerful effect on her—that while he was so good at eliciting information from her, he'd given virtually nothing away about himself.

The more she'd thought about it, the more she had started to wonder who the real Jaco Valentino actually *was*. Just who lay behind that darkly handsome exterior.

But the moment she had laid eyes on him again those doubts had been knocked aside like skittles—washed away by the tidal wave of attraction that had all but taken her legs from under her.

So after the christening ceremony, when Jaco had pulled her to one side, saying that he had a proposition to put to her, Leah's senses had gone into free fall.

Taking her by the hand, he had led her into one of the many echoing rooms of Castello Trevente, the grand property that was now her sister's family home. But his proposition

had taken her by surprise. Instead of pulling her into his arms and making mad passionate love to her right there and then, up against the hard stone walls of the *castello*—something that Leah had been fantasising about ever since she had met him—Jaco had calmly offered her a job at his vineyard. He needed a marketing manager with immediate effect. He thought she would be perfect.

Quickly hiding her surprise, Leah had jumped at the chance. All her good intentions, her vague misgivings, had been instantly forgotten. A job in Sicily was a dream come true after the tedious boredom of Glenruie, the small town where she had been born and bred and had spent most of her adult life trying to escape. Capezzana was warm and exotic and beautiful. And so was the man who owned it. The thought of working alongside Jaco, spending more time with him, had only made his offer all the more enticing.

So Leah had moved to Capezzana straight away, with Jaco joining her for the first few days to help her settle in. Showing her around the grand *palazzo*, he had casually told her to treat it as her home, to choose whichever rooms she wanted for her offices and accommodation—as many as she liked.

Because it was the vineyard that was Ja-

co's real passion—that was evident in the way his eyes lit up when he discussed the type of grapes they grew, last year's harvest, the quality of the wine they produced.

Leah had been left in no doubt about what Capezzana meant to him. And, in turn, how much faith he was putting in her by giving her this job. She had determined there and then that she wasn't going to let him down. She would work hard, learn fast and prove to Jaco, and to herself, that she wasn't the flighty air-head that some of her stupid decisions of the past would suggest. Show him that his faith in her had not been misplaced.

On his last night there they had been sharing a simple supper outside, watching the sun setting over the vines, when finally it had happened. *Finally* the storm of desire that had been steadily building between them for so long had broken.

Starting with a bruising kiss, they had been tearing at each other's clothes within seconds, stumbling backwards into the *palazzo* in their haste to find a bedroom, breathlessly surrendering to their craving hunger with wild, reckless abandon.

And so it had started—their stop-start relationship. Blisteringly hot nights of passion

interspersed with long periods apart when Jaco was jet-setting around the world.

A billionaire tycoon with the Midas touch, his packed portfolio meant that the demands on his time were enormous. Leah had learnt to accept that that was just the way it was. And, despite the passionate nature of their relationship, they had both kept it light, had concentrated on living for the moment, having fun.

For Leah's part, it was all about self-preservation—trying to hold herself back, refusing to let herself fall for this enigmatic man. And Jaco… Who knew what lay beneath that darkly compelling charm? Sometimes Leah wondered if he was just too preoccupied, too mercurial, too damned busy with his own big-shot career ever to belong to anyone.

Yet as she looked at him now—the living, breathing embodiment of him, instead of just a heated memory in her mind—and he gazed at her with those midnight eyes, he managed to make her feel as if she was the most gorgeous, most treasured creature ever to set foot on this earth. As if she was all he could ever want.

The fragile hope that she had so carefully repressed bloomed into life. Maybe, in view of what she had to tell him tonight, their relationship *could* become a much more per-

manent arrangement. Maybe they could be a proper couple…a family.

There was one sure way to find out…

'Actually, Jaco…' Leah took in a deep breath. 'There is something I need to talk to you about.'

'Sí?'

But already Jaco was distracted, dropping his bag to retrieve the phone that was buzzing in his trouser pocket. Leah watched as, his head bent, thick dark curls gleaming, his thumbs flew over the keypad. *That bloody phone.* It was like an instrument of torture. She would wait weeks to see Jaco, only to find herself competing with the wretched thing. And if not that, some other form of electronic communication.

He looked up. 'Sorry, what were you saying?'

The phone buzzed again and, pulling an apologetic face, Jaco started to tap out another reply.

'Scusa.' He was still concentrating on the screen. 'I have to reply to this.'

Of course you do.

'I'll tell you what…' Leah sighed with exasperation. 'Why don't I fix us some food while you finish what you have to do?'

'Buona idea.' He picked up his bag again and slung it over his shoulder. 'I'll have a re-

ally quick shower.' That wickedly slow smile put in another appearance. 'Unless you want to join me, of course? In which case it could take a bit longer.'

The phone in his hand buzzed again. Leah scowled.

'Ten minutes.' He dropped a kiss on her lips before turning away, putting the phone to his ear. 'Then I'm all yours.'

Leah stared after him, at his arrogant height, the broad set of his shoulders, the play of muscles beneath the handmade shirt. And somewhere inside her she felt her heart twist. Because deep down she wondered whether that could ever be true.

The ten minutes stretched into fifteen... twenty. Sitting out on the terrace, watching the golden sun lengthening the shadows of the vines as it started to sink below the horizon, Leah pushed aside her bowl of untouched pasta. Picking up a piece of bread, she absent-mindedly threw a few crumbs to the sparrows pecking around her feet.

This was typical of Jaco—always so busy, always clinching one deal or chasing after another. Always keeping her waiting. Even though her job kept her occupied, and even though she loved it, it still felt to Leah as

if her time at Capezzana was time spent in limbo—just waiting for Jaco to reappear.

But tonight he was here. And, even though he didn't know it yet, she was about to get his full attention. Telling him he was going to be a father was huge—momentous. She had no idea how he was going to take it. She hadn't begun to get her own head around the idea—yet.

With a heavy sigh, Leah pushed back her chair and went inside, where the only sound was coming from the overhead fan circulating the warm air. Was Jaco still in the bedroom?

Her bare feet made no sound as she crossed the old tiled floors towards the rooms she had occupied since moving in here. With their French doors, opening out onto a small terrace, she had picked them over the many other empty bedrooms upstairs, liking its cosy feeling of a small apartment inside this rambling *palazzo*. Liking, too, the way Jaco always automatically headed there when he visited—as if her space was his.

Despite herself, her mind began conjuring up images of him still naked from the shower, of his smile when he saw her, of the way he would take her in his arms and make love to her, all thought of food forgotten. All thought of what she had to say to him forgotten—at least for a short while. She knew she had

absolutely no willpower as far as Jaco was concerned.

With her hand on the doorknob of the bedroom, she hesitated. She could hear Jaco speaking. Yet another business deal, no doubt.

Silently turning the handle, she had only opened the door a fraction when some sixth sense kicked in, telling her that, no, this was *not* a business conversation. Through the crack in the door she could see him, sitting on the bed, his back to her, a laptop balanced on his knee. He was taking a video call, and the woman on the screen was dark-haired, dark-eyed…beautiful.

A cold finger of dread traced Leah's spine. Speaking in Sicilian, their voices were soft, Jaco's little more than a whisper, but there was no mistaking the tone—tender, caring, the sort of tone that lovers shared.

Leah forced herself to try and understand what they were saying over the deafening thud of her heart. Her command of the language was pretty basic, but Jaco seemed to be telling her not to worry, that everything would be all right.

'*Lo prometto*, Francesca.'

I promise.

But it was their final words that left no room for doubt. Paralysed with dread, Leah

watched as the woman touched two fingers to her lips and blew Jaco a kiss, smiling tenderly as she told him she loved him. And Jaco's reply shattered Leah's world into a thousand pieces there and then.

'Ti amo anch'io...'

I love you too.

She turned away, blinded by tears, numbed by the shock that was slowing her heart, closing her throat.

How could she have been so stupid? How could she ever have thought that she and Jaco might actually have a future? How could she have been taken for a fool by a man again—only this time a thousand times worse, a thousand times more painful?

Retracing her steps, she fled back out onto the terrace, descending the steps that led down into the private garden, running through the archway in the yew hedge and out into the vineyard itself. Racing through the rows of vines, she just kept going, running and running, the heavy bunches of grapes swinging as she rushed past, her breath burning in her chest. She had no thought for where she was going. No thought for anything other than that she had to get away.

CHAPTER ONE

One year later

'No!' JACO STARED at his friend in disbelief.

'It's true, Jaco.' Vieri's voice was deadly calm. 'I wouldn't be telling you this if it was just gossip. In fact, I'm not supposed to be telling you at all. But I thought you had a right to know. You have a child—a son.'

'No!' Jaco repeated, banging his fist down on the bar top, his eyes wild.

Vieri picked up his drink, silently regarding Jaco over the rim, waiting for the shock of the revelation to sink in.

'And what makes you think it's mine?' Dragging in a desperate breath, Jaco rounded on Vieri.

'Leah has told Harper that the boy is yours. I see no reason why she would lie. Especially as, far from hounding you for maintenance, it seems she doesn't want anything to do with you.'

'So how old is he, this child?' Covering his face with his hands, Jaco pulled them away again to reveal his horror.

'Three months, apparently.'

'Three months?' He gave a low growl.

'Yes. Does that seem…?' Vieri hesitated, choosing his words carefully. 'About right?'

'About *right*?' Jaco threw the words back at him, fury tainting his voice. 'Trust me, Vieri, nothing about this seems *right*.' He jerked himself to his feet, sending the bar stool rocking.

'Calm down, Jaco.' Vieri placed a steadying hand on his shoulders. 'I know this has been a shock, but it doesn't have to be so bad.'

'Doesn't it?' Jaco glared at him, eyes wild. 'And you'd know, would you?'

'I have a son, and I know he's the best thing that ever happened to me. That and Harper, of course.'

'Well, good for you and your happy little family.'

'Jaco!'

'Trust me, Vieri, you have no idea how bad this could be.'

Nobody did. Nobody knew anything—not even Vieri, his oldest friend. It was far too dangerous. Now this discovery could blow the whole thing sky-high.

Vieri shrugged. 'Okay, have it your own way. But don't shoot the messenger.'

'I'm sorry.' Begrudgingly, Jaco nodded an apology. 'So where are they? Leah and this son of mine?'

'That I don't know.'

'Don't give me that.' Jaco's anger quickly resurfaced. 'You are lying.'

Getting to his feet, Vieri squared up to his friend. 'I don't appreciate being called a liar.' His voice was deceptively soft. 'Especially when I'm trying to help you.'

'Help me?'

'Yes. I didn't *have* to tell you any of this. I've had to go behind Harper's back, and that's not something I'm proud of. But, like I say, I thought you had the right to know.'

'So Harper—she knows where Leah is?'

'No, she doesn't.' Vieri glared at him. 'So don't even *think* about pestering her for information. She only found out about the baby herself very recently. Leah has kept the whole thing hushed up.'

The two tall, handsome Sicilian men squared up to each other again, hostility simmering between them, until eventually Vieri put his hand on Jaco's shoulder again.

'Look, why don't you sit down and have another drink—take a few minutes to calm

down?' He signalled to the barman to refill their glasses. 'I take it from your reaction that you had no idea?'

Jaco gave him a haunted stare, but accepted the glass Vieri held out to him, seating himself back down on the bar stool.

'So when did you last see Leah?'

'Ages ago.' Jaco raked a desperate hand through his hair. 'Last August, maybe? Yes, it was just before the grape harvest. It was then that she told me she was quitting her job.'

'She didn't say why?'

'No. She disappeared for hours on the first evening I was back at Capezzana, and when I finally tracked her down she went all weird on me. It was getting late so I thought I'd leave her to it, try and get some sense out of her in the morning, but by then she had packed up and left—disappeared without a trace.'

'And you didn't try and find her?'

'No, Vieri, I *didn't* try and find her.' He glared angrily at his friend. 'She made it quite clear that we were done. The job…us…'

'Hmm…' Vieri stared into his glass. 'So there was an *us*?'

'Well, yes. We'd been seeing each other for a few months—nothing serious.'

'Well, it has clearly had serious consequences.'

Jaco pinched the bridge of his nose, then dragged in a breath. 'I've got to find her, Vieri. I mean, right away. If Harper *does* know where she is…even if it's just a guess…'

'Don't push it, Jac.' Vieri's eyes held more than a hint of warning. I've told you—she has no idea where Leah is.'

'Then I'll just have to find her for myself.' Pushing himself off the bar stool again, Jaco started for the exit. But at the door he stopped and retraced his steps, pulling Vieri into a rough hug. 'Thanks, Vieri. I can see this has put you in a difficult position. I appreciate it.'

Vieri gave him a slap on the back. 'That's okay. I just wish I hadn't been the bearer of such unwelcome news. I hope you manage to sort things out.'

'So do I.' Jaco jammed his hands into his pockets. 'So do I…'

Leah awoke with a start. There was a faint sort of scratching noise coming from the front door. Heart racing, she slipped out of bed and glanced into the crib, where Gabriel was sleeping peacefully, before moving silently into the living area of the tiny apart-

ment she had called home for the past few months.

The noise was coming from the other side of the front door and now, as she strained to listen, she could just make out whispered male voices. *Oh, God!* Someone was trying to break in.

She turned, stumbling back towards the bedroom, where her phone was on the bedside table. But it was too late—she didn't have time to get there. With the force of a tornado suddenly they were in, beside her, their terrifying presence filling the small room.

Her scream was instantly muffled by a large hand clamped over her mouth, pulling her back against a body built like a brick wall. She fought wildly, kicking out behind her, desperately flailing her arms to try and attack him until he easily pinned them to her body with an arm of steel around her chest.

Panic surged through her, and the powerful instinct to protect her baby son overwhelmed every other thought. Somehow she would get rid of these thugs. Somehow she would talk her way out of this.

It seemed there were two of them—one holding her prisoner, the other shutting the door behind them, then moving over to the window and pulling back the curtains a cou-

ple of inches to look out onto the street. Only then did he switch on the overhead light and come to stand before her.

Jaco! Leah stared at him in utter astonishment.

A relief of sorts washed over her, but it was short-lived. One look at his harshly drawn face, the cold determination in his eyes, and her worst fears came crowding in. He must have found out about Gabriel. He had come to claim his son.

'Yes, it's her.' Jaco nodded, speaking in Italian to the brute who still had his hand clamped across her mouth. 'The boy must be in there.' He looked over his shoulder.

Leah squirmed wildly, making the vice-like grip around her tighten still further.

'Don't fight it, Leah.'

He swung his gaze back to her, finally making eye contact. Leah gasped beneath the restraining hand. The familiarity of those eyes, now emanating such chilling intensity, was almost enough to stop her pounding heart.

'You and the baby are leaving with us. Right away.'

Leah roused herself, widening her eyes, shooting him as much poisonous venom as she could possibly muster. No way was he taking them anywhere.

'I will instruct Cesare to remove his hand, but only once I know you are going to be sensible.' He waited, his gaze fixed on her face, coldly assessing her. 'Can I trust you?'

Leah nodded frantically, and after a second's pause Jaco gestured to his minder.

Leah screamed. As loudly as her panicked lungs would let her. It was an ear-piercing shriek that echoed off the walls and saw a hand clamped firmly over her mouth again. Only this time it wasn't the minder's—this time it was Jaco's.

'Big mistake, Leah.'

His face was only inches from her own, and his powerful frame was pressed up against her so that she could feel the heat emanating from him, sense the barely leashed rage that held him so taut, shone in his eyes.

'If you want to do this the hard way, we will. But for all our sakes I suggest that you do as you're told. It will be far simpler in the long run.'

Leah glared back at him, blinking against the hot, seductive whisper of his breath fanning across her face, using her eyes to impart as much anger and determination and bravery as was possible when she was sandwiched between two muscled men.

She stared into Jaco's deep brown eyes—

eyes that had mesmerised her from their very first meeting. The memory of them had haunted her for weeks after she had fled Sicily. But now those eyes stirred something else in her—something gut-wrenchingly deep and primal. For it was like looking into the eyes of her son—the exact same shape, the same colour.

Gabriel was a miniature version of his father. And it was that that made her lungs, already struggling to keep her alive, threaten to give up altogether.

'I am going to give you one more chance.' He delivered his ultimatum softly. 'When I remove my hand you are going to remain silent while I tell you what is going to happen. Is that understood?'

Leah nodded. What choice did she have?

Very slowly, Jaco peeled his hand away from her mouth.

'There—that's better.'

He still stood within a couple of inches of her, watching her intently, his eyes fixed on her mouth as if willing it to stay closed. Leah felt the burn of his gaze on her lips, felt them swell as the blood returned to them, twitch with something other than fear.

'You can let go of her, Cesare. Go and stand by the door.'

With a grunt of obedience her captor released her and moved away.

Leah let out a gasping breath. 'What the *hell* do you think you're doing?'

The words came out in a torrent of fury, but Leah kept her voice low, mindful of Jaco's warning, and even more mindful of the fact that he was standing between her and the bedroom where Gabriel was still sleeping. With her mind racing in all directions she desperately tried to figure out a way of distracting Jaco so that she could go to Gabriel, scoop him up and run away with him—and keep on running until she woke up from this nightmare.

But this was no bad dream. This was horribly real. As the heavy breathing of the man mountain who was guarding the front door behind her reminded her. Not to mention the arrogant specimen of manhood who had planted himself before her.

'I've told you—you and the baby are leaving. Go and pack a bag.'

Leah shook her head in disbelief, furrowing her brow as she stared at him. 'Jaco, this is ridiculous. Have you taken leave of your senses?'

Jaco gave a low growl. 'I can assure you my senses are perfectly intact. Now, do as you're told.'

'But—'

'Five minutes, Leah. You have five minutes to gather your belongings.'

'And if I refuse?'

'Then you will be leaving with nothing. Because you and the baby are coming with me, either way.'

'So you are kidnapping us? Is that it?' Her voice shrieked with rising hysteria.

'I prefer to call it removing you to a place of safety.'

'Safety?' Astonishment stiffened her spine. 'We were perfectly safe *here*, until you crashed in.'

'No, you weren't, Leah.'

'What do you mean? Of course we were.'

'I am not prepared to discuss this now. You are under my protection and you will do as I say. Go and pack.'

Putting his hands on her shoulders, he turned her in the direction of the bedroom, the touch of his fingers burning against her bare flesh.

'And hurry up about it.'

Leah stood in the dark room, listening to the sound of her baby's soft breathing and the thud of her own heart. This was complete madness. Her eyes quickly darted around, but there was no escape from here. The apart-

ment was on the fourth floor of a high-rise tower block, and the only window offered nothing more than a view of the sleeping London skyline.

Working on autopilot, she pulled a suitcase from the wardrobe and started to stuff in some of her clothes. Then opening a drawer, she took out Gabriel's baby clothes, plucking more little vests and sleepsuits off the drying rack beside her and shoving them in the case too.

In truth, she had very few belongings. Since coming to London nine months ago she had moved more times than she could remember, going from one dank and dingy room in a grotty shared house to another, finding jobs wherever she could to try and make ends meet, before finally swallowing her pride and signing on for state benefits.

When the council had found her this flat—literally days before Gabriel had been born—she had wept with relief. It wasn't much, but it was a home, and that meant everything to her.

'Are you done?'

She turned to see Jaco silhouetted in the doorway, all dark, menacing authority.

'Jaco, why are you doing this to us?' She walked towards him, keeping her voice calm, firm. If there was one last chance to stop this

madness she was going to seize it. 'If you will tell me what's going on I'm sure we could work something out between us.'

'*Could* we, now?' Sarcasm scored his voice.

'Yes—why not?'

'Because I have no interest in working things out with a woman who has been so deliberately deceitful…' his gaze fell on the sleeping baby in the crib '…that she has kept from me the fact that I am a father.'

'Jaco… I…'

'Save it, Leah.' He raised his hand. 'You will have plenty of time to explain yourself later. First we are getting out of here.'

'But where are we *going*?' She was pleading now.

'You'll find out soon enough. Give me your passports.'

'Passports?' A fresh wave of panic washed over her.

'That's what I said.' Jaco fixed her with a punishing stare.

'No—you're not having them.'

'Hand them over, Leah.'

'No.' She squared up to him. 'You can't make me.'

'Keep me waiting any longer and you will find that I can.'

Leah glared at him in desperation. What-

ever had happened to the charming man she'd once thought she knew?

'Jaco...' She tried again. 'Why are you behaving like this?'

'Passports.' He held out his hand impatiently. 'Now.'

With no alternative but to do as she was told, Leah ducked past him and, going into the tiny kitchen, opened a drawer and took out two passports, holding them against her chest. Too late she realised she could have lied—told Jaco that Gabriel didn't have a passport. The only reason he had one was because she had wanted to be prepared for any eventuality—including fleeing the country to get away from Jaco if necessary.

Over the past twelve months Leah had spent far too much time thinking about Jaco Valentino—he had crowded her head, pervaded her thoughts day and night as if there was no escape from him. Finding out he was a cheating, two-timing bastard had broken her heart, and if that wasn't enough a darker worm of doubt had begun to eat away at her. About his background, his business dealings, the sort of people he associated with.

She had found herself remembering things that had barely registered at the time. The skilful way he had avoided talking about his

past, for example, and the set of his jaw—just a little too firm—when she had threatened to pry too much. His obsession with work—constantly checking his phone, working late into the night…

On more than one occasion she had come across him at two or three in the morning, having stealthily removed himself from her bed, his fingers flying across the keyboard of his laptop, a look of grim determination on his face. With the laptop hurriedly closed at her approach, she had politely but firmly been ordered back to bed, any attempt to ask him what he was working on dismissed with a kiss on the lips before she had been shepherded away.

In retrospect, his need for privacy had been excessive, and now Leah had another word for it—*secrecy*. Jaco was a man with secrets. She didn't know what they were. But something told her they were bad.

Which was why she had made the decision to flee to the anonymity of London, to keep her pregnancy a secret, to tell no one about Gabriel. The more she'd examined Jaco, the more convinced she had become that she had to protect Gabriel from him at all costs. As long as he didn't know of his son's existence, Jaco could do him no harm.

Doing it alone had been *so* hard, but keeping the secret from her twin sister had been the hardest thing of all. Harper was used to Leah packing up and leaving on a whim—usually chasing a dream that never materialised. So she hadn't been that surprised to hear her sister was on her travels again.

Keeping it deliberately vague, Leah had rung her every now and then, assuring her that she was fine, that she was having the time of her life, in fact, and then ending the call and sobbing her eyes out.

Somehow she had managed to keep the pretence going through all those long, lonely months. But deep down she had always known she would crack in the end—and crack she had. Just recently, after yet another mind-numbingly sleepless night with the baby, she had reached for her phone, scrolled to her sister's number and, taking a shuddering breath, called and confessed to her about Gabriel.

Fending off the barrage of concerned questions, Leah had kept the details to a minimum, saying that he was Jaco's child, but that she wanted nothing whatsoever to do with him. That under no circumstances was Harper to say anything. She had sworn her sister to secrecy.

And look where that had got her.

Leah's eyes travelled from the passports in her hand to the implacable face of the man who was waiting for them. With a shaking hand she passed them over to him.

'There. Happy now?' She tried for defiance as she watched Jaco flick through the pages, his grim features hardening still further as he found the grainy photo of his baby son.

'Gabriel *McDonald*.' He spat out the name in disgust, barely leashed anger holding him taut. He looked up, thunder clouding his face. 'This is *my* son, *my* flesh and blood—' he jabbed at the photo with his finger '—and yet not only did you not see fit even to tell me of his existence, but he bears *your* name.'

'Yes, he does.' Leah flinched beneath his furious scrutiny, but she refused to show her fear. 'And that's because I don't want you to have anything to do with him.'

Jaco gave a hollow laugh. '*That* much I had worked out for myself.' He speared her with his eyes. 'But let me assure you, Leah, your solo rights over this child are very much at an end. The child's name *will* be changed—this passport *will* be changed.' He held it aloft. 'My son is a Valentino and that is the name he will bear.'

Leah felt a wave of panic surge inside her.

This was exactly what she had been dreading—Jaco storming in, taking over. As a proud Sicilian man, family meant everything to him—she knew that.

From the few scraps of information he'd thrown her she had managed to piece together the fact that his parents had died when he was five, that he'd lived in a children's home for several years, along with Vieri, and then been adopted at the age of eleven. She knew he was estranged from his adopted family, but any attempt to find out why had been met with a chilling refusal to say any more, Jaco's urbane mask slipping, ever so slightly, to reveal a darker, more shadowy side.

But his heart was firmly embedded in the small Mediterranean island that he called home—that much was obvious. She had seen it in his eyes when they had been at Capezzana, heard it in his voice. And Leah had no doubt that with such lineage came the primitive sense of possession, the unilateral decision that *his* child would live in *his* country and obey *his* rules. To him blood ties were the strongest tie of all—binding. Impossible to break.

'Jaco...' In desperation she cast about, looking for some reason. 'Can't we at least *talk* about this?'

'No.' He closed the space between them. 'The time for talking has passed. I have no intention of standing here listening to your pathetic excuses. I don't want to hear anything you have to say. From now on we are going to do things my way.'

He towered over her, backing her up against the kitchen cabinets, the passports still held aloft in one hand as his eyes raked over her body.

Leah swallowed. Everything about the taut strength in his powerful body, the glint of steel in his eye, the granite set of his jaw, told her there was to be no reasoning with this man. And yet still his nearness provoked a reaction in her that was wholly inappropriate, tightening her nipples, tensing her core.

And, worse still, Jaco could see it. As his hot eyes darted over her defensive figure, lingering on the swell of her breasts beneath the skimpy vest top, they left a shuddering trail of havoc in their wake and Leah could sense his masculine satisfaction. His realisation that he could still do this to her, that his control over her took many forms.

But maybe she could use it to her own advantage. With a wild surge of adrenaline Leah imagined reaching out to him, linking her arms around his neck and pulling him

closer, finding his lips, kissing him, having him kiss her back. Because despite everything she still wanted that kiss. Despite everything she had gone through in the past twelve months, everything she had so sternly told herself, she still wanted Jaco.

For a moment he gazed at her—as if reading her thoughts, as if he knew exactly what was going on in her head. Then with a slight curl of his lip—a gesture so deliberately dismissive that it curdled Leah's stomach—he looked away.

'Get some clothes on.'

Leah watched as he stowed the precious passports in the inside pocket of his jacket.

'We are leaving.'

Fleeing to the bedroom, Leah pulled on a sweatshirt and a pair of jeans, picking up her phone and slipping it into her handbag. Then, bending over the crib she gazed down at her baby son, still sleeping soundly through all the drama. Her heart swelled with anxiety and pride.

With his arms flung out on either side of his head, his little fists closed, he looked as if he was ready for a fight, ready to take on the world. But Leah knew that was *her* job—that she would do absolutely anything to protect him, to keep him safe. Even if right now that

meant scooping him up and taking him God knew where, obeying the orders of a man who, she now realised with dread in her heart, was far darker and far more than dangerous than she could ever have imagined.

Reaching for the baby sling, she slid it over her head, holding Gabriel against her shoulder as she lowered him into it, tucking him in so carefully that he barely even stirred.

'You are ready?'

Jaco had silently come to stand beside them—the closest he had ever been to his son. Leah held her breath, waiting to see how he would react, expecting him at least to want to take a peek at the small, dark head pressed snugly against her chest. But instead he turned away, checking his watch and then picking up her case before leading them out of the room.

As Leah closed the door to her apartment behind her she realised she had no idea what was happening or where she was going. No idea when she would ever be back here again.

CHAPTER TWO

LEAH LOOKED DOWN at her baby son's head. The furious suckling of a few minutes ago was easing off now as he had almost had his fill. She rocked him in her arms—more to comfort herself than him. Gabriel was perfectly happy. He had his mother and a convenient source of food and that was all he needed.

He didn't have the slightest concern that the two of them had been abducted, spirited away in the night. Bundled first into a limousine that had driven them to an exclusive apartment block, then whisked up to a helipad on the roof, strapped into a waiting helicopter, piloted by Jaco himself, and finally landing several hours later at wherever on earth it was that she found herself now.

Exhausted by shock, she had dozed off on the flight, only waking as the helicopter had banked steeply in preparation for landing. Peering through the window, she hadn't

been able to make out anything at all in the darkness, and it had been clear that Jaco had no intention of telling her where they were, so she'd had to let herself and Gabriel be helped into a Jeep and just watch in stupefied silence as Jaco got into the driver's seat and navigated the steep and twisty road that had led to the residence she now found herself in.

But at least now it was daylight. Once she had Gabriel settled she would take stock of her surroundings and work out where on earth she was. The GPS on her phone should tell her that—when she managed to find it, that was. She had searched everywhere for it last night, with no success.

From looking around her, all she had managed to ascertain was that they were staying in some sort of luxury single-storey dwelling. Her bedroom was all cool elegance, with exposed stone walls and polished hardwood flooring, and a bed big enough to accommodate a small family. The en suite bathroom was of grey marble and had a sunken tub and succulent cacti growing behind a glass wall, while the floor-to-ceiling windows offered a view of a carefully landscaped garden, with ancient olive trees and time-worn granite boulders left in situ, but not much else.

A sharp tap on the door made her jump.

'Yes?' She hugged Gabriel closer to her.

The door opened and Jaco strode in. Wearing faded jeans low on his hips and a sleeveless black vest, he was all masterful authority. That was until he caught sight of Leah holding Gabriel to her breast.

'Oh…my apologies.'

Leah fixed him with a haughty stare. She wasn't going to look away. Breastfeeding a baby was the most natural thing in the world. And besides, she was perfectly decent. 'What do you want, Jaco?'

Jaco hesitated, then moved into the room, towards the chair where Leah sat with Gabriel. Leah noticed that his eyes did not quite meet hers, or move to the bundle of baby in her arms, but hovered somewhere over her shoulder.

'I came to see if you had a comfortable night.'

'Huh!' Leah snorted. 'Like *you* care.'

Her sharp voice made Gabriel's eyes flicker beneath the paper-thin skin of his closed lids. When his mouth fell from her breast Leah adjusted her clothing, and then moved to settle him in the crib by the side of the bed.

She had no idea how that crib had got there. She couldn't imagine it being the sort of thing

Jaco would have had stashed away for the convenience of his guests, but miraculously it had been there when they had arrived last night, along with disposable nappies and other essential baby equipment.

'I obviously care enough to be asking you now.' A muscle twitched beneath his eye. 'Do you have everything that you need?'

'Oh, yes, *everything*.' She flashed him a combative stare. 'Everything apart from my freedom, of course.'

'You will have your freedom.' Jaco matched her glare. 'All in good time.'

'And when might that be?'

'A couple of weeks.'

'A couple of *weeks*?' Leah advanced towards him like an impending storm. 'You really think you can keep me and Gabriel hidden away here for two whole weeks?'

'I don't think—I know. I can keep you here as long as I like.'

'And you believe that's acceptable behaviour, do you?' Leah inhaled a furious breath. 'Gloating over the way you can hold us prisoner?'

Jaco shrugged. 'I believe the bounds of acceptable behaviour have already been crossed. Not bothering to tell me I am a father, for example.' His eyes held hers.

Leah scowled. 'You are not fit to be called a father—not in the true sense of the word.'

A couple of angry steps brought her right in front of him, but her bare feet gave Jaco even more height advantage than usual.

She threw back her head to look up at him. 'You try to make out that being a father is so important to you, and yet you haven't even looked at Gabriel. Not once.'

Jaco ground down on his jaw. 'I will make my son's acquaintance when I feel the time is right.'

'Make his acquaintance?' Leah openly mocked him. 'You don't make your baby son's *acquaintance*, Jaco, you pick him up, hold him—*love him*.' Her voice quavered with unwanted emotion. 'Something you know nothing about.'

'Is that right?'

His fingers curled possessively under her chin, holding it firmly so she had no choice but to look into his eyes.

'And what leads you to that conclusion?'

'I… I just know.' Caught in the spell of his gaze, Leah couldn't think straight. All she knew was that no matter how badly Jaco behaved, how much she despised him, her heart still performed a crazy little dance whenever he touched her. 'Call it instinct.'

'Instinct be damned.' Jaco dropped her chin in disgust, moving a step away. 'You and I both know the real reason I am not at ease with my child is because up until a week ago I didn't even know of his existence.'

'And you still wouldn't if I had any say in it.'

'Esatto.' Jaco's voice fell to a deadly low tone. 'Which is why you no longer have any say in it, *mia cara*. From now on I make the rules, and I call the shots. What I say goes.'

'And I'm supposed to accept that, am I?' She glared at him incredulously.

'You have no choice.' He was chillingly calm. 'You can try and fight this all you like—kick and scream to your heart's content. But the outcome will be the same. You will not be leaving this island until I say so.'

An island. They were on an island. Amid the bubbling rage Leah stored away that piece of information, though she had no idea what good it would do her.

She tried to steady the anger that was coursing its fiery path through her veins. No mean feat, given the outrageous barbaric behaviour of the man in front of her. Hot-headed by nature, her instinct was to do all the things that Jaco had just described so dismissively. Kick and scream and beat her fists against this heinous man's chest. But she was also

clever. And she was a fighter. If it was clear that raging against Jaco was going to get her nowhere she would have to try another tactic.

Squaring her shoulders, Leah met his gaze full-on, cursing the kick of desire that he still triggered in her, that refused to die, no matter how much she tried to kill it.

'Well, at least you could do me the courtesy of telling me *why* you have kidnapped us—what we are doing here. You owe me that.'

'I owe you nothing, Leah McDonald.'

Leah bit down hard on her tongue. In her book this arrogant, hateful man simmering before her owed her everything. Her life as she knew it, her aching heart—her sanity, come to that. Everything that had been destroyed when their paths had so fatefully crossed. When he had seen fit to blow her world apart.

'So what is going to happen after this so-called two weeks, then?' She fought to stay calm, not to rise to his bait, plumbing the depths of a composure she hadn't known she possessed. If she wanted to find out any information she had to keep her head. 'How do I know that you won't keep me and Gabriel here for ever?

'Because that would serve no useful purpose.' Jaco's infuriatingly penetrating gaze burned into hers. 'And, despite what you

might think, I am not doing this solely for my own entertainment.'

'Well, what am I *supposed* to think?' The tide of anger rose fast again, creeping up her neck, flushing her cheeks. She looked away, snatching in a breath to try and compose herself before returning her eyes to his again.

'Frankly I couldn't care less *what* you think. Your opinion of me is of zero interest. But you have my word that your stay here will only be for a couple of weeks.'

'Your *word*?' She gave him the full force of her contempt.

'Yes, Leah, my word.'

Leah hesitated. 'And then what?'

'Then I will be putting plans in place for the future.'

'And what does *that* mean?' A curl of dread unfurled inside her.

'You'll find out soon enough.'

'So I was right.' Blood rushed to her head. 'You are never going to let us go, are you? You are going to keep us captive for ever, move us around from place to place, keep us locked in some squalid basement so that we never see the light of day—like those horror stories you read about in the papers.'

'For God's sake calm down, Leah.'

Jaco closed in on her with a single step,

catching her against him and restraining her hysterical rant with two hands placed firmly on her bare shoulders. Leah felt the heat of his touch sear into her skin, branding her flesh, causing her nipples to tighten.

'I will *not* calm down.' She went to twist away but Jaco held her firm, coming closer until the minuscule gap between them disappeared completely.

'Well, get some control over your vivid imagination, then.' He moved one arm around her shoulder in a blatant display of masculine dominance. 'Getting yourself worked up is not going to help anyone. There will be no moving around, and no basements. Circumstances mean that unfortunately it is necessary to keep you here for a short period of time…'

'Circumstances?' Fighting to free herself from his arms, Leah threw back her head so that her auburn curls rippled down her back. '*What* circumstances?'

'But while you are here,' Jaco continued, as if she hadn't spoken, 'you will be offered every convenience to make your stay as pleasant as possible.'

'Let me assure you, Jaco Valentino, there will be nothing remotely *pleasant* about my stay.' Her reply whistled through the air like a bullet.

'No?' Jaco let his eyes slowly drift over her face, watching as she blinked to try and hide her reaction to him.

Her muscles twitched beneath her heated skin…her mouth pulled into an unconscious pout. She hated the way he could do this to her. Hated even more the way he revelled in his power.

'You're sure about that, are you, Leah?'

'Yes—yes, I am.' She stepped away from him, backwards into the room.

'Well, I guess I will just have to take your word for that.' His tongue pushed against the inside of his cheek. 'Anyway…' He turned an arrogant shoulder. 'I just came to see if you needed anything. There is plenty of food in the kitchen if you would like to join me for breakfast.'

'I would rather boil my head in oil.'

'Suit yourself.'

She watched, breathless with burning impotence, as Jaco moved towards the door, deliberately rolling his shoulders as if to be rid of her, the tanned olive skin stretching over his muscled torso.

Reaching the doorway, he stopped, leaning against the doorjamb to address her again. 'Oh, by the way…' He feigned a casualness belied by the intensity of his stare. 'If you are

looking for your phone, I have had to requisition it. Just for the duration of your stay.'

'You have done *what*?' Speechless with anger, Leah could only gape at him. He must have come into her room and *stolen* it from her. This was unbelievable.

'I can't afford for you to give away your whereabouts and I don't trust you to keep quiet.'

Too right she wouldn't keep quiet. She had already planned to GPS her location and ring Harper, the police, Interpol—anyone that would listen to her. Now all those options had been snatched away from her.

As she watched Jaco stride away it hit her like a blow to the head how utterly defenceless she was. How totally she was under his command.

Jaco marched down the corridor, intent on putting as much space between him and Leah McDonald as quickly as possible. He needed to get some air into his lungs, clear his head.

His problems had started the moment he had walked into her bedroom—a big mistake, as it turned out. The sight of Leah nursing the child had broken his stride, made him falter. Something about the way her head had been bent, her auburn curls tumbling over the ba-

by's face as she rocked him very gently from side to side, had had a visceral effect on him, striking him like a blow to the chest.

They had looked so natural, so perfect, so innocent. The tender scene had captivated him for a split second, before quickly solidifying like cement, weighing him down with bitterness and anger. Because Leah *wasn't* innocent. Far from it. She was manipulative and clever. She had used those skills to hide the fact that she was pregnant with his child. To keep him from his son.

Jaco had no idea why she would do something so cruel, so heartless. Clearly he had got her wrong.

From the short time they had spent together he would have described her as many things: funny, intelligent, strong, sexy, unpredictable. But not manipulative or underhanded. And certainly never cruel. It was true that his friend Vieri had warned him she was trouble, but Jaco had laughed it off, preferring to make up his own mind about people. But it seemed Vieri had been right. Ms McDonald was not who she appeared to be.

But she was the mother of his son. And, as such, Jaco intended to use this time to find out everything he could about her. He would

be keeping a very close eye on her—both now and in the future.

Breakfast forgotten, Jaco picked up his laptop and headed for the terrace, settling himself under the shade of the sail-shaped awning. He scanned the view only briefly before settling down to work. He wasn't here to admire the scenery.

Although this island was supposed to be his own personal piece of paradise, so far he had spent no more than a handful of days here. The villa had been finished more than a year ago, but somehow he'd never managed to find the time to enjoy it. Not that that bothered him. It was a sound investment—as was the island itself.

One of several islands he owned off the north coast of Sicily, this was the one he favoured most. Dramatically beautiful, it had fine, dark-coloured sand—a result of centuries of volcanic activity. One day he would take the time to enjoy it, but not yet. Right now he had other things on his mind.

He scrolled down the long stream of new emails, scanning them quickly for information. Everything appeared to be progressing as planned. Proceedings would soon be reaching the most critical stage. Everything he had been working towards for so long was

finally about to come to fruition. Finally—*finally*—his vile adopted family were going to get what was coming to them.

The organisation, the meticulous planning, the months of painstaking work that had gone into this scheme were finally going to pay off. His legal father, his so-called brothers, his uncles—the whole damned lot of them—were going to get caught. No mistakes, no one slipping through the net. It was all or nothing.

Jaco had masterminded the whole plan, and his determination to bring his abominable corrupted family to justice coloured his every waking moment. Luckily he knew their biggest weakness—greed. He also knew that to stand any chance of winning he had to play them at their own game. So, with the backing of international drug enforcement agencies and the Italian police, who had been trying to bring the Garalino family to justice for years, Jaco had set up a daring sting operation.

Using the dark web and bitcoin—the preferred currency of the underworld—he had come up with a deal his family couldn't refuse: a massive cocaine smuggling operation. Under the cover of exporting olive oil to South America, and importing coffee beans to Europe, the cocaine would find its way into Sicily to be distributed around Europe. It was

a massively risky strategy—not least because only a few carefully prepared and positioned sample sacks would actually contain cocaine. Something his family wouldn't discover until they had fully implicated themselves.

The stakes were so high that if the sting went wrong—if they found out Jaco was behind it, which they undoubtedly would—he had effectively signed his own death warrant. But Jaco had calculated it as a risk worth taking. Francesca was safely in hiding. He was a single man with no dependents, so at least he would be their only target. And he could take care of himself.

But now everything had changed. He had a son. And Jaco knew he had to take immediate steps to protect him.

As far as he was concerned you didn't cross your family—or if you did you could expect reprisals of the very worst kind. Family on family. With no mercy. And, like an unprotected baby bird in its nest, Jaco Valentino's infant son would be seen as a prime target.

Behind him he heard Leah walking down the corridor towards the kitchen, the angry slap of her sandals on the marble floor. Even though she was clearly ignoring him, he instinctively closed the lid of his laptop. Sitting back, he spanned one hand across his forehead.

If the Garalinos ever discovered he had a son, Gabriel would be in immediate danger—even without the sting operation. Merely by virtue of being Jaco Valentino's son he would be of great interest, seen as a possible weakness in Jaco's armour, a way of paying him back for leaving *the firm*.

Jaco had had nothing to do with his adopted family since the age of eighteen, when he had finally managed to escape their clutches. His only regret was that he hadn't been able to take his younger sibling with him—not then.

Leaving Sicily, he had moved to New York, started a new life, and successfully built up a business empire that had rapidly made him a billionaire. A combination of astute intelligence, an unerring nose for a great deal, plus more than his fair share of good looks and easy charm, had got him far.

But beneath the urbane exterior and the effortless manners lay a very different man. Although he had made his home in many different countries his heart had always remained in Sicily, and slowly he had returned—anonymously at first, but then, as his wealth and power grew, with more authority, buying land, property and, most significantly of all, the Capezzana vineyard.

Capezzana had been in the Valentino fam-

ily for generations. It had been Jaco's family home until the age of five, when his world had imploded. When both of his parents had died when their car had plunged over a cliff. Jaco and his younger brother, who had been only a toddler at the time, had been taken into care, and finally adopted by the evil Garalino family when Jaco was eleven.

Although Capezzana had been left to Jaco in his parents' will, he'd had no claim on it until he was eighteen, so it had been run by a co-operative trust for several years—as the Garalinos had known it would be. This had been their chance to infiltrate the business and put into practice the nefarious schemes that Jaco's parents had so steadfastly refused to comply with.

Their bravery had eventually led to the 'unfortunate accident' that had seen their car plunge over a cliff.

The co-operative had been no match for the notorious Garalino family, and soon the prized Capezzana wines had been adulterated by harmful chemicals, and inferior wines had been relabelled and sold to investors at vastly inflated prices. The Garalino family had got rich quick and their greed had known no bounds.

Luigi Garalino had decided that to have

total control over the vineyard he would need to do something about the Valentino boys before the elder one came of age. So he'd come up with a master stroke: he would adopt the two of them. As their legitimate parent he would be able to oversee Capezzana legally for the next few years—plenty of time to induct them into the ways of the Garalino family. And a couple of healthy young boys were always useful in his line of business. The elder one in particular, a strong lad of eleven, had looked to him as if he might be a useful asset.

Wine production at Capezzana had gone into overdrive, with the Garalinos churning out hundreds of gallons of adulterated wine—far more than the land could ever produce. But their greed, as ever, had been their downfall. The government had got suspicious and eventually requisitioned the estate. But with friends in high places the Garalino family had never been prosecuted, and Capezzana had been left to fall into ruin.

That was until Jaco had got involved. After lengthy negotiations he had finally managed to buy the estate back from the government and his inheritance had finally been his. It had taken years of hard graft, but now it was prospering again, its reputation restored. And of all the businesses in his packed portfolio

Capezzana was far and away the one of which he was most proud.

Jaco knew full well that the Garalino family would be watching him, tracking his movements. But he had never openly crossed them, never even hinted to anyone of the depths of their depravity—not even his closest friends—and so far they had left him alone, kept their distance, bided their time.

What they didn't know was that they were about to walk into his trap.

These were extremely dangerous times. Jaco had had no alternative but to scoop up his son and bring him here. It was imperative that no one knew of his whereabouts—of his existence at all. Which meant that Leah had had to be seized too. Gabriel could hardly be separated from his mother at this age.

Like it or not—and Jaco most certainly did *not*—he was stuck with Leah McDonald until the Garalino family were safely behind bars.

He could hear her now, moving about in the kitchen, clattering crockery. And despite his decision to ignore her, to get on with the pile of legitimate work that needed his attention, he found he couldn't concentrate. Rising to his feet, he headed for the kitchen, somehow drawn towards this woman against his will.

She didn't hear him approaching—she was too busy studying the coffee machine, trying to figure out how it worked. Wearing a simple sunshine-yellow cotton dress, she had tied her hair up in a high ponytail so that it swung back and forth as she bent her head this way and that, pressing buttons and pulling levers. She appeared much younger than her twenty-seven years, with her jaunty hair and long, lightly tanned legs, and for a moment Jaco felt a stab of guilt for bringing her here. For unwittingly dragging her into the messy, complicated drama that was his life. For having altered the course of her life so completely. Maybe she had the right to dislike him as much as she obviously did.

'Here—let me.' Moving towards her, he saw her start, then defiantly tip up her chin at his offer of help.

'I can do it myself, thank you.'

'Sorry—my mistake.' He stood deliberately close to her, perversely enjoying the way his nearness was unsettling her. 'I take mine black, two sugars.'

Leah scowled at him, then scowled at the machine, before thrusting the bag of coffee beans into his hand. 'Fine, *you* do it.'

Jaco took charge, and soon the room was filled with the smell of freshly ground cof-

fee and the gurgling sounds of the dark liquid brewing.

Handing Leah a cup, Jaco watched as she sat herself down at the sleek glass dining table. 'Help yourself to breakfast. There's yoghurt, honey, muesli, loads of fresh fruit.'

'I'll stick with coffee, thank you.' Leah glared at him over the rim of her cup. 'Funnily enough, I don't have much appetite.'

'Just as you like.'

Jaco went to the fridge and took out a pot of yoghurt and spooned some into a bowl, then selected a peach from the fruit bowl and sat down. He could feel Leah's eyes on him as he started to slice the peach, but she looked away as he put his thumb in his mouth to suck off the juice.

'But it must be important that you keep up your strength—for the baby, I mean. Where is he, by the way?'

'He is asleep in the bedroom.' Leah's chest rose with violent indignation. She was immediately on the attack. 'And don't you dare start telling me what I need to do when it comes to my son.'

'Okay, okay.' Jaco held up his hands in surrender. He took a mouthful of yoghurt, but in truth he had no more appetite for breakfast than she did.

'And he has a name, you know.' Leah hadn't finished with him yet.

'Ah, yes, Gabriel.' Jaco sounded the name slowly, letting his tongue rest behind his top teeth on the last syllable. 'The name I had no say in choosing.'

He thought he saw a flicker of guilt cross Leah's face, but she remained silent.

'But I have to say you have made a good choice.' As her guilt turned to surprise Jaco felt a sense of satisfaction at the way he had wrong-footed her. 'Gabriel is actually my father's middle name. Or maybe you knew that?'

'How on earth would I know that?' She recovered herself with the scornful reply.

'A fortuitous coincidence, then.' Jaco cut another slice of peach and offered it to Leah on the knife. She shook her head as if he were offering her poison. 'Giacomo Gabriel Valentino. I was named Giacomo after him, but my name got shortened from a very early age. Still...' He ate the slice of peach himself, then set down the knife. 'It will be good to have another Gabriel Valentino in the family.'

Leah shot him a glance, opening her mouth to protest, then closing it again, sensing that this was a battle not worth fighting. And she was right. Jaco was very possessive about names. Forced to take the Garalino name

when he'd been adopted, he had changed it back to Valentino as soon as he had come of age. Valentino was his true name—the name of his parents. His son would be a Valentino, and in turn *his* son too.

At the time the Garalinos had tried to stop him, but by clever manipulation Jaco had made sure that he got his way, slowly easing himself out of their clutches, using logic rather than anger, cunning instead of violence. Trying to appease them had half killed him, but it had been important to draw as little attention to himself as possible. They were still watching him, of course—Jaco was under no illusions about that. But not for much longer. Soon vengeance would be his and his life could start again.

A life that now involved a child—his son.

Jaco roughly ran a hand around the back of his neck. He still hadn't come to terms with the fact that he was a father. Somehow he didn't know how to process it. He still hadn't held his son in his arms. Anger rose inside him again that Leah could have kept something so momentous from him. And, worse still, could sit there now, looking at him with disgust, as if *he* was the one at fault. He had absolutely no idea what was going on in her head.

Perhaps it was time to find out.

CHAPTER THREE

Leah watched as Jaco stretched out his arms, then placed his linked hands in his lap. He leant back, crossing one long leg over the other at the knee, his posture relaxed, but his expression one of fixed determination.

She felt her insides shrivel, mourning for the man she had thought she knew—the witty, charming, fun-loving Jaco who had stolen her heart. But even now—even faced with this new, formidable, baffling version of him—she couldn't stop her pulse quickening, her body from thrumming with forbidden need. Despite everything, she knew she still wanted him.

'So.' The fingers of his clasped hands twitched. 'In view of the fact that we share a child, perhaps it's time I knew a little more about your family.'

'There's nothing to know.' Leah immediately went on the defensive.

'It's just you and Harper and your father, *sí*?' Jaco ignored her. 'I remember you saying that your mother died when you were young. Twelve, wasn't it?'

'Yes.'

Leah was *not* going to feel flattered that he remembered. That balmy evening on her first visit to Capezzana, when they had cosily shared some of the details of their lives seemed like a massive mistake now. The compassionate way Jaco had looked at her as she'd told him of her mother's tragic shotgun accident, reaching for her hand and holding it in his lap, now seemed as fake as everything else about him.

In retrospect she wished she'd kept her mouth shut. Instead, sitting there sharing a bottle of delicious Capezzana wine, watching the fireflies darting through the night, she had blurted out her whole life story: her mother's death, her father's descent into alcoholism, the shock and misery of discovering that she had kidney failure, the four years of dialysis before she had been able to have a transplant, her twin sister being the selfless donor.

Yes, she had told him everything. At the time it had seemed like the most natural thing in the world. It was only later she had realised

how little Jaco had divulged about *his* background, *his* family. Now she could see that he knew everything about her and she knew nothing about him.

'And how is your father?' Jaco wasn't letting the subject go.

'He's fine, thank you.' Leah's reply was clipped to the scalp. But at least it was true. Angus McDonald had been sober for well over a year now.

'And does he know about Gabriel?'

'No, he does not.' She pulled her ponytail over her shoulder, twiddling the hair between her fingers.

'So your sister is the only person you have told?'

'Yes.' Leah glared at him.

'And you can trust her to keep quiet?'

'No, I can't!' Jumping to her feet, Leah moved over to the window, then swung round to confront him again. 'Because if I *had* been able to trust her she wouldn't have told *you* and Gabriel and I wouldn't be in this mess!'

Leah was going to have *very* strong words with her sister when she next saw her. That was assuming she ever saw her again.

'Actually, it was Vieri who told me.'

Ah, yes, of course—that figured. Old friends watching each other's backs.

'He, at least, recognised that I had a right to know.'

Leah gave him a silent scowl.

'So—and this is very important, Leah—can we establish that, apart from ourselves, Harper and Vieri are the only two people who know that Gabriel is my son?'

'Yes,' Leah hissed back. 'We can *establish* that.'

'Well, that's something, I suppose.'

She saw his broad shoulders flex as he reached to pick up his coffee cup. Leah tensed. Why was he so obviously relieved that no one else knew about his son? Suddenly it felt like a personal slight against her and against Gabriel.

'So you can see your dirty little secret is quite safe.' She sniffed haughtily.

'My son is *not* a dirty little secret.' Jaco was on his feet in an instant, towering in front of her. 'Far from it.'

'Really? Then how come you don't want anyone to know about him?'

'I have my reasons,' Jaco replied. 'But when the time is right I will be only too proud to show him to the world.'

'*What* reasons, Jaco?' Leah glared at him in frustration. 'Why can't you tell me?'

'Because you are better off not knowing.'

Leah stared at him, his chilling words seeping into her bones. He turned stiffly from her, but it was too late. His curt statement had already given him away. Not for the first time, it occurred to Leah that Jaco Valentino might be involved in something bad. *Really* bad.

She was still staring at him when he turned back, his harsh features pulled back into line.

'In any event…' He looked at her with cold disdain. 'You are hardly in a position to criticise me for wanting to keep Gabriel a secret. You haven't exactly been shouting his arrival from the rooftops.'

'No.' Leah glared back. 'Because I have my reasons too.'

'So go on, then. Explain them to me.'

'That's easy.' Leah hurled the words at him like a grenade. 'Because I have discovered the sort of man you really are.'

A flash of shock fleetingly crossed his face before his expression hardened, like quick-setting concrete, all emotion banished.

'Meaning what, exactly?'

Leah forced herself to meet his gaze, not to look away again. Something about his stiffened posture, the sharp light in his eyes, had betrayed him. Oh, yes, he was trying to cover it up with intimidation now—all hard-angled jaw and imperious scowl—but it wouldn't

work. It was too late. She didn't know what nefarious plans he was trying to hide, but she *did* know he was a two-timing cheat. And that was more than enough to damn him.

She bit down hard on her lip to stop the avalanche of pain that threatened to break through the fragile walls of her self-control. Being faced with him like this hurt so much. All the suffering he had put her through—the heartbreak, the loneliness and terror of giving birth so completely alone, then trying to cope with a newborn baby—was welling up inside her, waiting to be released in a torrent of misery and bitter recriminations.

But she had got through it—she had survived. And now she had Gabriel and he was the most wonderful blessing in the world. He was the only thing that mattered, in fact.

She took in a breath. Was there any point in confronting Jaco with his infidelity? Would it actually achieve anything? Or would she just be exposing her own weakness, her own hurt? Another thought occurred to her. Maybe the fact that she had discovered this other woman could be used to her advantage at a later date. Saved as some sort of painful trump card. Because at the moment it certainly felt as if Jaco held the entire deck.

'I'm waiting.'

She looked up, having almost decided to keep her counsel. But as she caught the fierce glint in his eye all reason, all logic, was suddenly drowned out by the beat of blood in her ears. He was looking at her as if *she* were the guilty one here. Looking at her with something bordering on disgust. How *dared* he?

'Very well.' She leapt to her feet, tossing back her head so that her ponytail swung across her bare shoulders. 'I will tell you the reason I chose to keep Gabriel a secret from you. I did it because…because…'

A buzzing sound stopped her in her tracks. His wretched phone was going off in his pocket!

'Un momento.' Holding up his hand to silence her, Jaco retrieved it, briefly scanning the screen before swiping to accept the call. 'We will continue this conversation very shortly.'

Without a second glance, he put the phone to his ear and strode from the room, speaking in rapid Sicilian that Leah had no hope of understanding.

Unbelievable.

Left alone, Leah growled in helpless desperation. Jaco obviously cared so little about her explanation, about *her*, that a random

phone call was of more importance. Or maybe it wasn't so random—maybe it was the lovely Francesca. No doubt he would drop everything for her. *Literally everything.*

Shaking with miserable frustration, Leah forced herself to be strong. *You know what?* Her internal monologue helpfully cut in. *He's had his chance and he's blown it.* If Jaco had so little respect for her—if he was so arrogant as to assume he could pick up their conversation at any time of his choosing—she needed to teach him a lesson.

She was glad she hadn't blurted out the truth. From now on she was going to make sure that she didn't tell him anything.

Staring through the window, she watched him walking away, the phone still clamped to his ear. Having crossed the decking area, he started down some rocky-looking steps, rapidly disappearing from view.

What she wouldn't do to have access to a phone…

Leah looked around her. Her own phone had to be here somewhere—now might be her chance to find it.

After glancing quickly out of the window again, to check that there was no sign of him, she hurried out of the kitchen and down the corridor in the opposite direction to her room.

One of these rooms had to be where Jaco slept. And that was most likely where her phone was hidden.

She found his bedroom easily enough. At the far end of the villa, it was the mirror image of hers, except the view was open to the sea. For a moment Leah stood in the doorway, looking around. Something about being in Jaco's personal space was making her breath catch. As her eyes scanned the room she was aware of him all around her—his intoxicating male scent in the air, his expensive clothes scattered carelessly around. But it was the bed that drew her gaze, the tangled twist of the white cotton sheet, the way he had tossed several of the feather pillows on the floor, leaving just one remaining, still bearing the indent of his head.

Leah stepped over the threshold. She didn't have time to stand around. And she certainly didn't have time to let her imagination run riot, thinking of Jaco in that bed. Pulling herself together, she went into full search mode, opening drawers, looking in the wardrobe and under the bed.

It didn't take long because everywhere was completely empty. Apart from the bag he had obviously brought with him, he didn't appear to have any possessions here at all. Maybe

this wasn't even his villa. Leah didn't know anything any more.

She quietly moved into the en suite bathroom. His toothbrush was lying by the side of one of the twin washbasins, a razor sticking out of an unzipped wash bag. Guiltily Leah opened up the bag and peered inside. No phone in there. Neither was it in the cabinet or any of the empty drawers beneath.

She went back into the bedroom—it had to be here somewhere. Moving over to the bed, she looked under the pillow, then ran her hand along the underside of the mattress. If she could lift the mattress up, she'd be able to see better.

Heaving one corner of it onto her knee, she balanced there as she paused for breath. It was huge, and surprisingly heavy, and all this effort was making her hot. Bending her head, she peered underneath, squinting to see if there was anything vaguely phone-shaped under there.

'Checking for bedbugs?'

Leah pulled out her head with a start. The mattress dropped down with a thump.

Jaco was leaning against the door frame, one long leg crossed over the other at the ankle, the toe of his handmade leather shoe resting on the floor.

'If you want an invitation to my bedroom, you know you only have to ask.'

'Where is it?' Leah raged at him, not even bothering to try to cover up what she was doing, why she was there. His supercilious smirk had smashed through her paper-thin control.

'What?'

'You know perfectly well what—my phone.'

'Ah, yes…that.'

Easing himself from the door frame, he casually strode towards her. Leah's fury increased with every lazy step.

'I'm afraid you won't be getting that back until we leave the island.' He narrowed his eyes. 'But rest assured I am taking good care of it for you.'

Leah felt so angry she thought she might combust, right there in front of him, leaving nothing but a swirling spiral of smoke. Shooting Jaco a furious glare, she pushed past him and fled from the room, the need to get away from him suddenly more imperative than breathing itself.

Jaco stared after her retreating figure. For all her posturing, her show of defiance, he could see how vulnerable Leah really was. On the surface she was all blustering confi-

dence, still trying to give the impression that she had some control over her situation, when clearly she had none, but deep down he knew she was struggling.

It shouldn't have bothered him. He told himself that he need have no conscience as far as Leah McDonald was concerned. Considering the way she had treated him, she deserved no sympathy. But still she got to him: the flash of anxiety in her eyes, the way she bit down on her soft lip, nipping it under her teeth, the way she curled her hair around her finger for reassurance. It all affected him somewhere deep and low. Somewhere he had no intention of examining.

He ran a troubled hand over his jaw. He had known from their very first meeting that there was far more to Leah than might at first appear. Fun and light-hearted on the surface, she ran a lot deeper than her vivacious, carefree behaviour seemed to suggest. Persuading her to open up about her past during that first visit to Capezzana, he had discovered she'd been through a lot—not least health issues, with her kidney failure and the subsequent transplant.

It was one of the reasons he had resisted the immediate sexual spark between them—fought against it with all his might, actually—

and that had been some test of his willpower! But something had told him that this woman was different…special. That she deserved his respect. He had strongly suspected that when they finally did get together there would be no going back. And, boy, had he been right about that. Just not in the way he had thought.

Yet even now, despite everything he knew about her, Jaco found his body still thrummed for her, and his libido refused to accept what his brain was telling it: that Leah McDonald was nothing but trouble. One look from those flashing hazel eyes and his body was instantly gearing up for action, as if she was hot-wired to his groin.

He had recently worked out with a jolt of shock that he hadn't had sex with anyone for over a year—since the last night he had spent with Leah, in fact. He hadn't so much as looked at another woman—which was not like him at all. He'd told himself he'd had a lot on his mind. That once this wretched business with the Garalinos was over he would pick up where he'd left off.

Luigi Garalino. Just the evil bastard's name was enough to turn his stomach.

But he was nearly there. Soon all his careful planning would come to fruition and he would finally have the first part of his re-

venge. Not the revenge he might have chosen, perhaps—an extremely long and painful death would have been too good for Garalino, in his opinion—but seeing the entire family locked up for several decades would certainly be a good start.

Step two—proving that Garalino was responsible for the death of his parents—came next. Jaco was already well on the way to getting the evidence he needed, and once word spread that the family had all been arrested he was confident that his sources would start squealing like pigs.

In the meantime he would have to content himself with the knowledge that their reign of evil tyranny was at an end. And, best of all, that meant Francesca could come out of hiding. She could finally start her life over again.

Her life as a woman.

The long and painful medical procedures were over and Jaco's little brother, Franc, was no more. The skinny little waif who had been plucked from the children's home alongside him, who had been systematically insulted and abused by his adopted family, no longer existed. Instead a dignified and beautiful woman had been born.

And Jaco couldn't be more proud of his new sister. He couldn't wait to show her off,

to spoil her, to bring her back to Sicily. With the Garalinos' pervasive influence everywhere it had just been too dangerous for her to return to their homeland, and she had spent the last five years in exile in New York. But very shortly all that was going to change and Francesca would come home.

Leaving the bedroom, Jaco followed Leah back down the corridor, catching sight of the flash of her yellow dress before she turned into the living room. He was reminded of an angry bee, buzzing away from him. Or maybe a wasp in a jar would be more accurate.

It was clear that she was never going to accept the situation she found herself in. If they were going to be sharing this villa for the next couple of weeks, for the sake of a bit of harmony maybe he needed to find some way to placate her.

The obvious immediately sprang to mind—only to be firmly squashed down. The thought of angling his head to access the sweep of her exposed neck, trailing his lips up to her earlobe, breathing into her ear before letting his mouth travel to her lips… It was an extremely tempting one. More than tempting. He could almost taste the kiss, and the memory of how her mouth had felt beneath his was suddenly pulling at his groin.

Kissing Leah had felt amazing. Their sex had been amazing. How had it ended in this tangled mess?

He followed her into the living area, intent on finding some way to ease the hostility between them. Leah was standing quite still, peering down nervously at the wide strip of glass flooring that cut the room in half.

'It's okay—it's quite safe.' Moving to stand in front of her Jaco took a couple of hefty jumps on the glass to prove his point.

Leah flinched, backing away.

Jaco's mouth twisted into a smile. 'Come on.' He held out a hand to her, which she pointedly ignored. 'I promise you, you won't fall in!'

Designed by a brilliant young architect, this villa had some quirky features—especially as Jaco had given the guy free rein to do whatever he wanted. The swimming pool running underneath the villa was one of them, as was the idea of leaving some of the boulders in situ and carving them into seats, and having the decking hang over the edge of the cliff.

Jaco had been very pleased with his work. Clearly Leah was not such a fan. From a safe distance away, she was still looking at the sparkling water running beneath Jaco's feet as if it might surge up and suck her under.

'You're not scared, surely?' He couldn't resist issuing the challenge, winding her up.

'No, of course not.'

Tossing back her head, Leah brushed past him, stepping purposefully across the glass floor to the other side. Jaco noticed she didn't look down.

'There—happy now?'

Jaco raised his eyebrows. 'Being here isn't some sort of endurance test, you know.' He moved towards her. 'It would be better for all of us if you could just relax and accept the situation.'

'Better for *you*, you mean.'

'Why don't you try and think of it as a little holiday?'

'A *holiday*?' Like a bull before a red rag, Leah looked ready to charge. 'A holiday where I am forbidden to leave. Where I've had my phone stolen from me. Where I don't even know where I am!'

Jaco hesitated. He could tell by the fierce glint in Leah's eye that she was far too stubborn, too feisty, to let this drop. He needed to come up with some sort of explanation for keeping her here if he was ever going to get a moment's peace.

He raked a hand through his hair. 'I can appreciate this is a difficult situation for you.'

'*Can* you, indeed?' Her voice was laced with sarcasm.

'In terms of where you are, this is one of my private islands. And the reason you are here is simply to keep you and Gabriel safe. That's all you need to know.'

'No, it's not, Jaco.' She pouted angrily. 'I need to know a lot more than that. And I'm never going to shut up until you tell me.'

Jaco let out an exasperated sigh. He knew exactly how he would like to shut her up—by taking her in his arms and covering those velvet lips with his own, making her forget all about her furious demands in the most pleasurable way possible. But he put the brakes on—fast. He was standing too close to her—he needed to find some space.

'Look…' He tamped down the smouldering fire. 'If you want to come outside for a minute I will do what I can to explain.'

She didn't need telling twice. As Jaco slid back the glass doors she was right behind him, stepping out onto the wide decked terrace that ran the length of the villa, so close she was like his sunshine shadow.

She raised a hand to shield her eyes from the sun, scanning the view. No doubt she was trying to sight land, or maybe a boat that might rescue her. Jaco noticed that she had

also clocked his laptop, at the far end of the terrace under the awning. Well, she would have no joy there—even if she did manage to get her hands on it she would find it locked. Now, more than ever, Jaco was meticulous about security.

'Take a seat.' He gestured to one of the padded sun loungers lined up on the deck and waited for Leah to sit on the side of one of them before he did the same opposite her.

'While I can't tell you a great deal, what I *can* say is that I am in the middle of some very delicate negotiations.' He chose his words carefully, intending to tell her as little as he could possibly get away with. 'And these negotiations are reaching a critical stage.'

'So?' Leah frowned impatiently. 'What has this got to do with me and Gabriel?'

'The people I am dealing with are not honourable men.' Jaco fought to conceal his hatred. 'They would be keen to exploit any weakness they could find. If they were to discover I had a son, he could be a potential target.'

'A target for what?' Fear gripped her voice.

Jaco shrugged, unwilling to divulge any more.

'You mean he might be kidnapped?' Leah jumped to her feet, her hand at her throat.

Or worse.

Jaco refused to process what might happen if the sting backfired and the Garalinos realised he had a baby son.

'No harm will come to him here, on the island, I can assure you of that.' He stood up to face her.

'I don't believe this!' Colour flooded the column of Leah's neck, spreading to her cheeks. 'You are prepared to put our child in peril just because of some dodgy business deal?'

'It's rather more than that.' Jaco clenched down on his jaw. 'And may I remind you that up until a few days ago I had no idea I *had* a child.'

'So these are the sort of people you do business with? Thieves and crooks?' Leah was in full flood now, fire flashing in her eyes. 'Are your greed and ego really such that you are prepared to go to any lengths to feed them?'

Jaco met her furious gaze full-on. He was *not* going to be spoken to like this. 'You need to learn when to hold your tongue, Ms McDonald.'

Reaching forward, he circled her upper arm in his grasp.

'Or what?'

Leah pointedly stared at his hand and Jaco immediately released her, taking several steps

away, appalled by the way this woman could make him lose his self-control.

Leah shook her head as if vindicated by his action. 'What sort of man *are* you, Jaco Valentino?' Her eyes glittered with murderous scorn. 'Actually, don't bother to answer that. I don't even care. You can keep your horrible dark and devious secrets to yourself. Just don't expect me to be impressed by all this.'

She gestured dramatically at the beautiful setting around her. Despite himself Jaco found his eyes drawn to the hitch of her breasts beneath the cotton fabric.

'Because no doubt it has only been acquired through the misery of others, through dodgy deals or blood money…or *worse*.'

'I can assure you it has not.'

'Well, whatever… Right now I have no idea who you are—what you are capable of.'

'No.' Closing the gap between them, Jaco leant forward, blocking her with the height of his body. 'Maybe you don't.'

He caught the flash of fear in her eyes, mixed with a sort of stunned surprise. But if she was determined to perpetuate this bad boy image of him he would go along with it. Maybe it was the only thing stopping him from making an even bigger mistake. Taking her to his bed.

A sharp silence fell between them, broken only by the mocking call of the cicadas in the ancient olive trees around them.

'Let me past.' Her voice faltered, her bravado slipping. 'I need to check on Gabriel. Thanks to you, who knows what terrible danger he may be in.'

Frustration coursed through Jaco, hot and fierce. His instinct was to reach for her, to pull her close, make her see that he was doing this precisely to keep their son from danger. But Leah's shimmering hostility, the alarm on her face, brought him to his senses and he took a step away.

'You are safe here, Leah. I guarantee it.' If he could only make her believe one thing, he wanted it to be that.

'Yeah, right.' Leah swept past him, her head held high, her ponytail swinging behind her. 'If it's all the same to you, *I'll* be the judge of that.'

CHAPTER FOUR

LEAH FLED BACK to her room, rushing over to Gabriel's crib, her heart thumping as she peered into it, as if something terrible might have already happened to him.

But of course he was fine, sleeping peacefully, his mouth open in a soft O, the sweep of his long lashes dark against his soft skin.

It was a source of constant surprise and fascination to Leah that she could have produced something so wonderful, so perfect as her son. But, gazing at him now, she was forced to acknowledge once again that she wasn't the only one responsible for this little miracle, this warm bundle of life wrapped up in squidgy pink skin.

Jaco's DNA was very much in evidence in the dark curls, the almond shape of Gabriel's eyes, even in the set of his little mouth that had a sort of no-nonsense purse to it. There was no doubt about it—he was going to grow up to be his father's double.

In looks, anyway. Leah lightly ran the back of her finger over his downy cheek. She would fight with her dying breath to stop Gabriel from turning into the kind of man his father was. A devious, cheating manipulator. Someone who was totally ruled by money, power and greed. Who was prepared to put his own child at risk for the sake of some shady deal. Prepared to kidnap him—and *her*, for that matter—just to swell the coffers of his rotten empire.

And as for his sexual morality… There was yet another example of the depth of Jaco's depravity. What sort of man could conduct a passionate affair with her, take her to his bed, make love to her, treat her as if she *mattered* to him, when all the time he had another woman on the go? How could he have kissed her that night, held her in his arms, and then less than half an hour later been on the computer, telling someone else—that poor Francesca woman—that he loved her?

A cheating, low-life scumbag kind of a man, that was what. And no matter how much Leah tried to tell herself that finding out had been a blessing in disguise, that at least she now knew the kind of man he really was, it still felt like a blade plunged into her heart. A heart that would never recover.

Turning away, she looked for something to do. She might as well unpack her case. Moving to the wardrobe that ran along one entire wall, she hung up the couple of dresses she had brought with her, almost laughing at how ridiculous they looked in the enormous space. Sliding open the chest of drawers, she laid out their clothes—Gabriel's little vests and sleepsuits in the top drawer, her tops and underwear below.

Well, that hadn't taken long.

She put her hands on her hips and looked around. With Gabriel down for his morning nap, obviously totally unperturbed by the situation they found themselves in, it seemed she had time to spare and nothing to do with it. She had no phone to look at, and no computer or tablet to browse—her usual form of entertainment when she had a few snatched moments to herself.

She stared out of the window at the bright sun beating down on the landscaped garden. Such heat was almost unheard of where she came from. The west coast of Scotland was very beautiful in its own way, but more prone to stormy skies and rainbows than blistering summer days. It seemed a shame to waste all this sunshine.

Her thoughts turned to the swimming pool

she had seen outside—inside too, come to that. Who would have a pool running *underneath* their villa? Jaco Valentino, that was who. Although she had to admit it was a pretty cool idea.

She felt foolish now, for being frightened of walking across the glass floor. But it had taken her by surprise—and water was something of her nemesis. Since nearly drowning in a freezing Scottish loch at the age of five she had had a deep-rooted fear of water, and had never learned to swim. As a child she had screamed blue murder when her parents had tried to teach her, and as a teenager—when she might have found the courage to do something about it—her kidney problems had meant that she was either too sickly or medicated to be able to face it.

Now, though, she had no such excuse. Not that she was planning on jumping in the deep end, literally, but there was a beautiful pool out there and a scorching day to go with it. Better still, she had noticed that at the back of the villa, far away from where Jaco was working, the pool was nice and shallow, with gentle steps leading down into turquoise water. It had looked so inviting, and the thought of getting in there to cool off, to unknot some of the tension that had been gripping her ever

since Jaco had stormed back into her life, was too tempting to resist.

She'd seen a bikini mixed in with the underwear she'd just put in the drawer and, decision made, quickly pulled it on. Picking up the baby monitor and throwing a towel over her shoulder, she was ready…

Stepping into the blissfully cool water, Leah gingerly waded in up to her waist. The pool was actually deeper than she'd realised, but as long as she was still well within her depth she'd be fine. With the sun beating down strongly on her shoulders, she decided to cool them off under the water too. She hadn't put any sunscreen on, and as she had the sort of complexion that would burn before you could say *biscuit*, she knew she had to be careful.

She waded in deeper, so that the silky water ran over her shoulders. She bobbed up and down for a bit, then moved over to the side of the pool and, anchoring herself with one hand over her shoulder, let her legs float up in front of her and stared up into the blue, blue sky. This was heaven. Or at least it would be if her entire life wasn't such a mess.

Not for the first time, Leah wondered why it was that everything seemed to happen to *her*. Why she couldn't just live a normal life, like a normal person: get married to a nice

man, settle down, have a couple of kids, a decent job. Why was it that she always seemed to lurch from one disaster to the next?

Her twin sister, Harper, was a prime example of doing it right. Brilliant at school, never any trouble, she had always been the clever one, the responsible one, taking care of everyone after their mother died and then, the most amazing thing of all, saving Leah's life with her gift of a healthy kidney.

Whereas Leah… Her illness and her mother's death had affected her very differently, making her want to rage against the injustice of it all, and against her father too, for turning to drink when he should have been looking after them. Her schooling had been constantly interrupted by illness, so Leah had left with virtually no qualifications. Not that she cared. Who needed stupid qualifications, anyway, when there was a whole world out there to explore, and so many adventures to be had?

But most of her adventures had just landed her in trouble—usually because they involved deceitful men. She'd lost count of the number of scrapes poor Harper had had to get her out of—her last mishap being a classic example. Although that one had had a *very* happy ending for Harper, so Leah now decided to view it as a triumph.

Working in a nightclub in Manhattan, she had struck a deal with the handsome owner—one Vieri Romano—to act as his fake fiancé for a generous payment. Which would have worked out okay if she hadn't been stupid enough to give the money to some guy who'd promised to triple it at the casino, only to lose the lot.

So it had ended with Harper stepping in, yet again, to sort out her mess. Except this time the mess had taken an unexpected turn, with Harper and Vieri falling madly in love and living happily ever after. For once, she had inadvertently done something right.

But from now on she was done with making mistakes. Getting involved with Jaco Valentino had clearly been another classic error, but she had been blessed with the gift of a son, and having Gabriel meant she could never regret what had happened between them. She just regretted that Jaco wasn't the man she had thought he was. She grieved for the man she thought she had known.

Letting go of the side of the pool, Leah twisted round on her tummy and spread her arms out before her. How hard could this swimming malarkey be, anyway? It was high time she learnt. Apart from anything else, as a single mum it was her duty to learn for

Gabriel's sake. Supposing she ever needed to rescue him?

The thought was too awful to contemplate. But it did spur her on to try. Launching herself forward, she kicked her legs and tried to keep herself afloat with flapping arms. But it just wasn't happening. As she started to sink she reached for the bottom of the pool with her toes. It wasn't there—she was out of her depth. Her head went under, then came back up, and she gasped and spluttered in panic before going under again.

This was it. She was drowning.

Jaco knew exactly where Leah was. He'd made it his business to know. From the other side of the villa he had watched through the twin walls of windows as she carefully waded into the pool, taking her time, as if she wasn't too sure she liked it.

Jaco liked it—he liked it far too much—and his body immediately responded to the sight of her clad in nothing but a skimpy bikini.

Her figure had changed, he realised. She had a more curvy shape now—her hips more rounded, her breasts fuller, straining against the triangles of bright blue fabric. Jaco swallowed. He had always found Leah an incredible turn-on, but now…

He dragged his gaze away. Lusting after Ms McDonald was not going to do him any good. They were in enough of a mess as it was. And yet his body refused to obey him, the kick of sexual need still making its presence very much felt.

He turned back, relieved to see that her siren's body was now covered up by the water. He would leave her to it, go back and do some work—try and put this wretched woman out of his head for a couple of hours.

But he had no sooner opened his laptop again when he heard what sounded like a faint shriek. Leaping to his feet, he dashed to the window to see Leah's head disappearing under the water. *Dio!* What the hell was she doing?

Tearing off his jeans and vest, he plunged into the pool, diving underneath the villa and emerging on the other side, colliding with Leah's thrashing body as he resurfaced. Grabbing hold of her, he swam them both backwards into the shallow water. The whole thing had probably taken less than a minute.

Leah struggled to her feet, spluttering madly, water streaming from her face. She coughed violently, then took a gasping breath deep into her lungs. Only then did she turn to face her rescuer. Staring at her with a mix-

ture of concern and astonishment, Jaco stood before her in a pair of black boxers that the water had shrink-wrapped against his magnificent form. She hurriedly looked away.

'So.' Jaco caught her chin and lifted it gently, so she had no choice but to meet his eyes. 'Would you like to tell me what that was all about?'

'It wasn't *about* anything.' Leah pushed the hair that was plastered to her face out of her eyes. 'I was just teaching myself to swim.'

'You can't swim?' Jaco stared at her incredulously.

'No, not as such.' She turned away and started to wade out of the pool. Her foot was on the first shallow step when she felt Jaco's hands on her shoulders, turning her to face him again.

'Then why would you put yourself in danger like that?'

'I wasn't in danger.' Leah gave a contemptuous laugh. 'I would have been perfectly all right.' She shrugged his hands off her.

'Like hell you would.'

'If it boosts your massive male ego to come plunging in here, thinking you're rescuing a damsel in distress, then by all means go ahead.' She desperately tried to claw back some composure. 'But the fact is I could have coped perfectly well by myself.'

'Ha!' Jaco shook his head, glittering droplets of water flying from his hair, incredulity in his scowl. 'You are something else, Leah McDonald. You know that?'

But, as dismissive as his words were, irritation setting his jaw tight, his eyes were telling a different tale. Drawn to her semi-naked body, they seemed to travel rapidly over every inch of damp skin. Leah's stomach flipped beneath his blatant scrutiny, her nipples hardening as he lingered on the swell of her breasts before he finally raised his eyes to her face. With nowhere to hide, she could only glare back at him, heat flaring across her cheeks as she hastily adjusted the fit of her bikini top.

It was far too small—she knew that. Since having Gabriel, her modest breasts had swollen dramatically—something she hadn't fully realised until she'd looked down at herself now, at the bikini that had fitted fine when she'd bought it a couple of years ago, now struggling to contain her new shape.

Something that Jaco had clearly noticed too, judging by the very male gleam in his eye. She saw him swallow, turn his head away for a moment, then look back.

'You know what? I wasn't exactly expecting profuse declarations of your undying gratitude, but a simple thank-you might have been

nice.' He fixed her with a lingering stare. 'Do I not even deserve that?'

'Very well.'

Leah pushed back her shoulders, clearing her throat. She would say anything if it meant she could get away from him. Away from the torment of his glorious body. From the way he was looking at her, making her feel.

'Thank you.' She pouted at him. 'There—is that good enough?'

'Not really, no.' Jaco's eyes glittered dangerously. 'I can see I'm going to have to extract my own reward.'

With a flash of bronzed muscle he breached the small space between them, towering over her, blocking out the sun. And as his hands came to cradle her head, his fingers working their way through her dripping tresses, Leah froze, all breath extinguished and her lungs gripped by the same primal need that kept her rooted to the spot.

His head lowered and suddenly his mouth was on hers, his lips so silkily seductive that it was all she could do to stifle a whimper of longing. She had wanted this for so long—dreamed about it, railed against it, but had never, ever been able to ignore it. And suddenly she was returning the kiss, as if on some destructive automatic pilot, her whole

body succumbing to the erotic sensations that his expert skills so easily aroused.

Moving his hands around her back, he pulled her closer to him, crushing her cold, damp breasts against the broad expanse of his chest, the slick of moisture sealing them together. As he caught the tip of her tongue with his, Leah responded, and the kiss grew more fervent, more passionate with every highly charged second. Such was his expertise, his sensual masculine power, the sheer perfection of him, that her senses were ripped apart, lost in the mad thunder of her heart.

Jaco slid his hands over Leah's wet skin, running them down her sides until they stopped at the curve of her waist, where they possessively spanned her midriff. *Dio*, this kiss felt so good. *She* felt so good. Holding her tight against him like this, he was at a loss to remember why she was so forbidden, why he couldn't just sweep her up into his arms, march straight back into the villa and make mad, passionate love to her.

He wanted her so badly it hurt. And not just in his groin, where the force of his erection pressed painfully against his boxers. His whole body thrummed for her, as if he had been struck with a tuning fork and the resonations had spread to every cell within him.

The thumb of his left hand felt the ridge of Leah's scar, and he softly traced the length of it, feeling Leah flinch beneath his touch. He knew she was self-conscious about the diagonal slash that ran south from her hip bone—the result of her kidney transplant operation. The first time they had been naked together she had tried to hide it, draping the sheet around her, but Jaco had gently removed it, wanting to see all of her, to learn everything her body had to tell him. In his eyes the scar was part of who she was, and it only made her more beautiful.

He shifted his position, breaking the kiss to alter his stance, as if that might somehow bring him to his senses. But it did no such thing. He pulled back far enough to look into the swirling depths of her tawny eyes, and what he saw there only served to throw more fuel on the blazing fire. There was wariness, a drugged sort of surprise, and there was something else—a deep, dark intensity that held all the promise and wonder of what might happen, what might be, if they let it. It was more than enough to tip him over the edge.

He lowered his head to cover her soft pink lips again, to lose himself in more of the heady pleasure of her mouth. His hands strayed over her behind, the skimpy fabric that barely cov-

ered her rounded buttocks clammy beneath his touch, sticking to her skin.

His breath hitched into the kiss. Leah had always had a fantastic body, model-slim, with legs that went on for ever. But now that body had taken on a new dimension, with soft curves replacing taut lines, the jut of her hips cushioned against his swollen groin and her breasts so plump, so full, that he longed to see them naked so he could fully admire their new, seductive shape. To see all of her naked, in fact. Because if Leah had been lithely sexy before—now she was irresistibly, off-the-scale, scorching hot.

Her arms had circled his neck and her fingers were laced, holding him firmly to her. It was all the encouragement Jaco needed. Moulding the hard planes of his chest against the cool, damp smoothness of her body, he reached for the knot of her bikini behind her back.

A distant moan permeated his consciousness. Was that Leah, or some guttural noise he had unwittingly made himself? He felt Leah start to move beneath the ring of his arms and reluctantly loosened his grip, realising that the sound was coming from neither of them, but from the baby monitor by the side of the pool.

Putting her hands against his chest, Leah pushed herself back, quickly looking down to check that her bikini was still intact.

Their eyes met briefly, Leah adopting a murderous scowl that was too little, too late. She had already given herself away. Jaco dropped his arms to set her free. But he refused to free her from the frenzied pull of desire between them. If *he* had to acknowledge the power of it, then so did she.

A highly charged second flashed between them before Leah turned away, hurrying back towards the villa as if her heels were on fire. Jaco stared after her, the sashay of that pert little derriere doing little to cool the blood that was still pumping manically through his veins.

The volume of noise coming from the monitor had ramped up considerably now, building to a full-blown throaty yell by the time Jaco had walked around the pool to pick it up and see a string of red lights flashing across the top. His son had a good pair of lungs.

Carrying it back towards the villa, he suddenly heard Leah's voice coming through, soft and reassuring, and the crying subsiding to a couple of snuffly grunts. Jaco stood where he was, listening to Leah's sing-song tone. There was something oddly compelling about eavesdropping on the tender exchange.

But unsettling too. Because it made him feel like an outsider—as if he would never be able to achieve even a fraction of the close and loving relationship that Leah and his son obviously already had.

Switching the monitor off, he strode into the cool of the villa and carelessly tossed it onto the nearest surface. When the time was right he would work out how to form a bond with his child. The enormity of being a father had yet to fully sink in, but the idea was slowly growing on him. Right now, however, he had too many other things on his mind. D-day was fast approaching. He had to keep his focus.

Going into the kitchen, he went over to the fridge to pour himself a glass of iced water. As the ice cubes rattled down he picked one out and ran it over his lips to cool their raging heat. Looking down at himself, he realised he'd need to sit in a bathtub full of the stuff the way he was going on.

He raked back his hair, silently growling with irritation. The riotous way his body had reacted to the sight of Leah's bikini-clad form was a distraction he could well do without. He was going to have to get that under control, and fast, or the next couple of weeks were going to get very complicated indeed.

CHAPTER FIVE

SITTING DOWN ON the rugged stone step, Leah cupped her chin in her hands and stared at the view. In the distance, framed by an azure sky and a deep blue sea, she could make out the shapes of two small islands, one further away than the other, both hazy against the sky and fringed with a white ring of surf.

Jaco might have refused to tell her exactly where they were, but Leah had worked it out for herself. On her first trip to Capezzana he had mentioned a string of volcanic islands that he owned off the north coast of Sicily, and how he would love to show them to her one day. He had probably forgotten he'd ever told her but, totally mesmerised by the enigmatic Sicilian, Leah had stored away every bit of information she had managed to glean from him.

As she gazed around her now, at the dark soil, the profusion of succulents and cacti, the exotic colourful flowers that thrived in

these fertile conditions, she knew this had to be where she was.

Not that the information was of much use to her. Short of putting a message in a bottle, she had no idea how to let anyone know of her plight. It wasn't as if she could swim to the nearest island. Anyway, it was probably uninhabited, or also owned by Jaco, or both. No, much as she had tried to fight against it, with every furious fibre of her being, she had to accept that she and Gabriel were prisoners here until such time as Jaco saw fit to set them free. Presumably when this hateful business deal had been concluded.

Giving a heavy sigh of frustration, she leant over to pick a bright purple flower, spinning it between her fingers before absently tucking it behind her ear. They had been holed up here for over a week now and, far from lessening, the pressure of being held prisoner was growing worse with every passing day.

The secrets that Jaco was so intent on withholding loomed larger in her head the more time she had to think about them. Because in Leah's experience, secrets were only there to cover up lies—the sort of lies that could hurt you...badly. Scarred for life by her first attempt at a relationship, she could hardly believe she had done it again—fallen for a scheming, lying

cheat. Only this time the drop had been a thousand miles deeper, a thousand times harder.

These were the thoughts that had haunted her for the past nine days and nights, accompanied at all times by the forbiddingly dark and brooding spectre of Jaco Valentino.

Somehow he managed to be both everywhere she looked and yet never actually sharing the same space. His formidable presence filled the air, putting Leah's fragile senses on high alert, whilst actually having very little engagement with her. In fact, since that kiss by the pool on the first day he seemed to have gone out of his way to avoid her.

That kiss.

The memory of it still shivered through her body. They had been apart for so long, and so much had happened, that Leah had genuinely forgotten the overwhelming power of it—the sheer, wondrous bliss of being kissed by him. She knew she should never have surrendered to it the way she had, that her body had betrayed her in the most blatant way, but how on earth was she supposed to resist? How could *any* girl not fall under his spell when subjected to such a gloriously erotic onslaught? Much as she told herself that she had to be strong, that she could resist him, *would* resist him, the fact was Jaco could still set her

on fire with nothing more than a slumberous glance from those hypnotic brown eyes.

So it was just as well that he was keeping his distance. The more he kept out of her way the better. She didn't want anything to do him—especially now she'd discovered that being a two-timing cheat was only one of his crimes. That he had a dark side that struck fear into her very soul.

She would just have to try to bide her time and survive the next few days, and then get as far away from him as she possibly could. Whatever else, she *had* to control her body's extreme reaction to him. Stop it from betraying her.

But how? That was the question. How did she stop her heart from banging in her chest whenever he walked into the room? Or leaping to her throat when he spoke to her? How was she supposed to react to the sight of his bronzed body, frequently stripped to the waist, as he wandered around the villa or strolled along the side of the pool, scooping up fallen leaves. Everything about his lithe movements, the flex of his muscles, the gleam of the sun on his dark curls—even the sound of his footsteps—sent her into a spin of craving and confusion that she had no command over at all.

Getting to her feet, Leah headed back up

the steps towards the villa. She never liked to stray too far from Gabriel, even when he had just been fed and settled and she knew he would sleep for at least an hour. The idea that there were people out there who might want to harm her baby son because of Jaco's corrupt business deals still made her feel sick. As did the fact that Jaco was the sort of man who would get involved with such people—worse still, was probably one of them himself.

But strangely—and this she didn't even understand herself—Jaco also made her feel safe. Deep down she knew that no harm would ever come to Gabriel while he was under Jaco's protection. Such was his authority, his total dominance, that she had no doubt he would have everything covered—every potential danger would have been anticipated and dealt with. Which, she supposed, explained why she and Gabriel were holed up here.

The villa was quiet when she stepped inside, her eyes taking a moment to adjust from the bright sunshine. She'd started towards the kitchen with the idea of making herself some coffee when something made her change her mind and she turned back towards her bedroom. Her heart stopped. The door to her room was wide open, yet she knew she had pulled it almost closed when she had left.

Adrenaline surged through her, speeding her silently forward until she reached the doorway, where she came to a sudden halt. There, standing with his back to her, looking down into the crib, was Jaco. Leah paused, waiting for her breath to steady.

She assumed he must have heard her approach—indeed that he would be able to hear the way her heart was banging with alarm. But as the seconds ticked by and he showed no sign of acknowledging her presence she realised she must be mistaken. He appeared to be so intent on studying the contents of the crib that he hadn't noticed her arrival at all.

Leah moved slightly to the side of the doorway so that she could observe the scene less obviously. She could hear Gabriel stirring now, recognised the shuffling sound of his legs kicking against the sheet before his little arms appeared, waving around with determined purpose. She watched as Jaco leant forward, her curiosity overriding her natural instinct to rush in and scoop Gabriel up herself.

'Ciao, piccolo uomo.' The words were softly uttered under Jaco's breath. *Hello, little man.*

Leah stared, spellbound, as Jaco tentatively held out a finger and Gabriel made a grab for it, grasping it in his fist.

'That's right.'

Leah could hear the smile in Jaco's hushed voice.

'I am your *papà*. Pleased to meet you.' He reached forward with his free hand to stroke Gabriel's curls lightly.

From her covert position, Leah watched, her breath hitched with surprise. Up until now Jaco hadn't shown the slightest interest in his son.

'Va bene.' Jaco rolled back his shoulders, almost as if he was having to psyche himself up. 'Let's pick you up, shall we?'

He paused for a second, before finally grasping Gabriel under the arms and lifting him carefully out of the crib.

'There we are.' He held him cautiously at arm's length, slowly turning him first one way and then the other, as if considering him from every angle. Front-facing again, Gabriel stared back at him, unblinking. 'You are a fine little fellow, aren't you?'

In response Gabriel started to kick his legs beneath him, but his eyes never left his father's face.

Jaco smiled at him. 'And lively too.'

Carefully transferring Gabriel to the crook of his arm, Jaco wrapped his arms around him so that he was nestled against his chest. 'There—how's that?'

Neither of them looked one hundred per

cent comfortable. Jaco's biceps were bunched way too hard for Gabriel's weight, making a pillow of stone to support his head. And his arms were wrapped so tightly around and under Gabriel that corded veins showed beneath his tanned skin. But, surprisingly, Gabriel made no move to escape. Apart from one leg, which he had kicked free to dangle over Jaco's arm, he seemed content to snuggle there, looking up at his father with something bordering on adoration in his eyes.

Leah sucked in a silent breath. She hadn't expected this—this visceral, deep-rooted response to the sight of her son in his father's arms. She couldn't explain what it was, knew only that it had weakened her bones, that if it hadn't been for the door frame she feared she might have slid to the ground. But still she couldn't stop staring at the two of them, mesmerised by the sight of their skin-to-skin contact, Gabriel's pale softness against Jaco's dark strength. Despite the awkwardness they looked right together—bonded. Almost as if this moment had been preordained.

Which was stupid.

Pulling herself together, Leah shook off the unwanted sentiment and pushed back her shoulders. Taking a deep breath, she stepped into the room.

'What do you think you are doing?'

She knew she sounded unnecessarily aggressive…snarky. She knew, too, that an agitated flush had spread over her cheeks.

Jaco looked up from where his gaze had been fixed on his son's face, meeting her eyes with deliberate calm. 'What does it look like I'm doing?' He threw down the words like a gauntlet. 'I am holding my son.'

'Well, don't.' Leah advanced towards him like the wind before a storm. 'I'm here now. I'll take him.'

Positioning herself in front of him, she held out her arms to take Gabriel from him, but clearly Jaco had other ideas.

Swinging the cradle of his arms to one side, he moved Gabriel out of her reach. 'All in good time.' He looked down at his son before raising his eyes to hers again. 'We are just starting to get to know one another.'

'Well, don't bother.'

The surge of emotion at seeing the two of them together had sharpened her tongue like a blade. She moved in front of them again, pointedly waiting for Gabriel to be transferred to her.

'It's no bother.' This time Jaco didn't move, standing his ground instead, like a bronzed statue.

'Really? Then how come it's taken you all this time to even pick him up?' Leah gave him both barrels. 'In fact, you have barely even looked at him.'

It had surprised Leah at first—Jaco's lack of interest in his son. She had fully expected him to take control of Gabriel the way he took control of every aspect of his life. To own him like a piece of property. But instead he had barely acknowledged Gabriel's existence, deliberately keeping his distance, looking the other way when Leah walked through the villa with Gabriel in her arms, avoiding the shady area on the decking where she had taken to laying out a rug to let him kick. In fact, during the whole, torturous nine days they had been together on this island, Jaco had never enquired after his son's well-being once.

Leah had told herself she didn't care. More than that, it was a relief. Pushing aside the niggle of hurt that Jaco could be so dismissive of something as amazing as their son, that he failed to see the wonder they had created and, by association, her part in that wonder, she had decided his indifference was actually a *good* thing. It was another reminder of why Jaco was a totally unsuitable father. Quite apart from his depraved behaviour, he was obviously a man with no heart.

'I admit it's taken me a while to get my head around the idea of being a father.' Jaco coolly deflected her ire. 'But don't forget I haven't had as long as you to get used to the idea.'

The implied meaning of his words hung between them, just as he had meant them to do.

'However, I'm starting to get used to it.' He looked down at Gabriel, who was wriggling now, and adjusted his arms to try and make him more comfortable. 'I have to say he is certainly a *bel bambino*.' He laid a protective hand over the top of Gabriel's head. 'Or what is it you say in Scotland? A bonny baby?'

Leah glared at him. His attempt at a Scottish accent was frankly dreadful. In any case, she didn't want him describing Gabriel in *any* language. She didn't want him to have anything to do with her precious son.

'I don't see any point in you trying to bond with Gabriel when your contact with him is going to be so brief.'

'*Mi dispiace?* I'm sorry?' Jaco raised cold eyes to look at her. 'Whatever makes you think that?'

'Well…' Leah forced herself to meet the glitter of his stare. 'I assume that once this wretched deal of yours is completed Gabriel and I will be free to go back to the life we

had before you kidnapped us. That you will leave us in peace.' She was trying for an air of superior sarcasm, but there had been more than a hint of desperation in there.

'Then you assume wrongly.' His gaze sharpened. 'I intend to play a full and active role in my son's life.'

'Right.' Leah gave him a mocking pout. 'And how exactly do you intend to do that when we live in different countries?'

A foreboding silence fell between them, punctuated by a small gurgle from Gabriel. Even before Leah had finished saying the words she felt the trap opening up beneath her, saw herself falling into it. She could only wait, with dread in her heart, to hear what might be coming next.

'I have been giving that some thought.' Jaco brushed a stray eyelash from Gabriel's cheek. 'And I have decided that Capezzana would be the best option.'

'The best option for what?' She really didn't want to hear this.

'For us to live in, of course.'

'Us?'

'*Sí*—you, me and Gabriel.'

'No!' Leah let out a gasp of shock. 'I mean there is no *us*.'

'I think you'll find there is.' He jiggled

Gabriel in his arms, already more confident with him.

'Don't be ridiculous. There is no way Gabriel and I are going to move to Capezzana—I can tell you that right now.'

'I seem to remember you jumped at the chance the first time I suggested it.' Jaco's reply was as smooth as silk.

'Well, yes, but that was different.' Leah cast around, looking for some sort of lifeline that wasn't there. 'At the time I needed a change. I needed a job.'

'And now you *have* a job. The most important job in the world, in fact. That of being the mother of my child.'

Leah felt the blood surge through her veins, and her palms itched to wipe that sanctimonious look off Jaco's infuriatingly handsome face. How dared he pontificate on the importance of motherhood? And what was all this *my child* business? As if he somehow had the right to dictate her behaviour.

'I don't need your patronising advice, thank you very much. Especially when you hardly know one end of a baby from the other.' She tossed back her head with such force that Gabriel blinked at her in surprise. 'You seem to be forgetting that I have actually lived and breathed the job for the past three months.'

'I know that.'

'No, you *don't*, actually.' She was on a roll now, picking up temper as she went. 'You have no idea…no idea at all…what it's like to be responsible for a newborn baby all on your own. How you worry about every little thing—whether he's too hot or too cold, whether he's feeding too much or not enough, whether those little spots really are just a milk rash or something much more serious. Whether you will ever get him to sleep and then…and then…' She took in a shuddering breath.

'And then what, Leah?' Jaco's eyes bored into her. 'Go on.'

Leah drew in a ragged breath. 'And then, when he finally does sleep through the night, the blind panic that comes over you that something terrible must have happened to him. The way your heart stops as you look into the crib, only starting again when you realise he is alive, when he is pressed against your chest, soft and warm and breathing.'

She stopped abruptly, realising she had said far too much, given herself away. Her hands flew to cover her hot cheeks.

A bruised silence settled around them as Jaco studied Leah's flushed face, searching deep into her eyes. The colour of autumn leaves,

those eyes had held a fascination for him from the start. The way they glowed with vitality when she laughed, shot sparks of fire when she was angry, darkened to a sultry heat when she was aroused. But now… Now they were clouded with strain and anguish, unwittingly revealing the terrors of the last few months, the sheer weight of the responsibility she had had to endure. *Alone.*

He sucked in a breath, the impact of that realisation pressing down on his chest. He had been so angry when he had found out about Leah's deception, so enraged that she could have given birth to his son without telling him, that he had failed to look at it from her point of view at all. Until now.

Did she really hate him so much that she had been prepared to endure any hardship rather than ask him for help? And, if so, why? After he had had to cut short their initial conversation on the subject, any further attempts to get answers from her had been blocked with furious contempt.

Not that it mattered now. Jaco couldn't do anything about the past, but he could determine their future. From now on he would be there for them, whether Leah wanted him to be or not. From now on Leah and his son would be his main priority.

'You are right.' He emphatically ended the silence. 'I did have no idea.'

He saw Leah bristle, her jaw tightening in readiness to do battle again as she fought to banish any trace of vulnerability. But he'd had enough of point-scoring, of trying to get inside Leah's head.

Bending down, he gently replaced Gabriel in his crib before turning to face Leah again. 'I can see that things must have been tough for you.'

'Well…yes.' Leah stared at him defensively.

'But all that is going to change. You are not on your own any more. From now on you have me to take care of you and Gabriel.'

'I never said we needed taking care of.'

'No arguments, Leah.'

'But…'

'I said no arguments.' Swallowing the space between them with a single stride, he took hold of Leah's chin, tipping it so that she had no alternative but to meet his determined gaze. 'You and Gabriel will be coming to live with me.'

As he spoke the weight of his words turned to certainty. He knew he was going to make that happen, no matter what. And as much as he told himself he was doing this for his son, and to ease the burden on Leah, deep down

he knew there was another, far more potent reason. He wanted Leah in his bed.

As he gazed at her now his hands itched to thread through her hair, to dislodge the purple flower that she had tucked behind her ear, accentuating her guileless beauty. He had noticed it straight away, that flower, and something about the frivolous gesture had speared his heart. It reminded him of the old Leah. The one he had known before she had been weighed down with responsibilities.

He let his eyes fall to her mouth and felt his breath stutter at the sight of her swollen pout, felt his control slipping still further as the powerful lurch of desire kicked in.

He had no idea how she did this to him, how all his resolve turned to dust whenever he was near her. He wanted to kiss her so badly he almost shook with it, but he refused to give in to his weakness. Not now. Now was not the time. For the time being he would have to content himself with the promise of things to come. Because he knew for certain that they would. The pull of attraction between them was far too strong to be ignored.

Letting go of her chin, he brought her into a hug. That way at least he was spared the pull of her gaze, the torture of her lips—he could almost convince himself he was doing it to

comfort her. Circling his arms around her in a close embrace, he was surprised when Leah didn't fight him, just let herself be held.

For a moment they stayed like that: Leah's head resting against his shoulder and Jaco breathing in the scent of her hair, feeling the effect ripple through his body like a glass of champagne. But the moment didn't last long. When Leah stirred in his arms he released her slightly, looking down into her tortured face.

'No, Jaco, I won't do it. I have fought so hard to make a life for me and Gabriel. I refuse to give up my freedom and independence now.'

'Freedom and independence?' Jaco threw her words back at her. No way was he going to accept that that was what it had been. 'To me it sounds more like three months of struggle and worry.'

'Well, of course there were times like that, but…'

'Not any more, there won't be. From now on I will take care of you both.'

'No.' She raised her hands to lever herself away from him. 'Gabriel and I can't move in with you. I can't let you take over our lives, determine our futures, just like that.'

'Yes, you can.' Taking her hands, he clasped them in his own, holding them against his chest. 'You can and you will.'

CHAPTER SIX

SITTING DOWN IN front of the mirror, Leah stared critically at her reflection. In the past she had always taken pride in her appearance, straightening her unruly auburn curls into a sleek curtain and artfully applying make-up to accentuate her eyes. But recently she had hardly given it a thought. What with all the stress of finding out she was pregnant and moving to London, she had had other things on her mind. And coping with a newborn baby had left no time for preening herself. Besides, what was the point? The only man in her life was Gabriel, and luckily he seemed to adore her no matter what she looked like.

But now she leant in for a closer look, frowning at the dusting of freckles that had appeared across her nose. They might be the unwanted result of nearly two weeks in the Mediterranean sun, but she had to admit her skin had a glow to it that had been missing

for months. Her eyes looked clearer too—less tired and sleep-deprived. For some unknown reason, Gabriel had taken to sleeping really well here, going right through the night for the last three nights in a row, which was almost unheard of.

Leah told herself that it was because it was so quiet—no police sirens or drunken brawls or thumping music from the neighbours. But somehow he just seemed altogether more settled, almost as if he had come home. Which was ridiculous. But it did mean that Leah had had more uninterrupted sleep than she'd had for a very long time and she knew she felt better for it.

Rooting around in her make-up bag, she found some bronze eyeshadow and mascara and set about applying them. A touch of blusher on her cheeks and some red lipstick and she was done. As she regarded her reflection again she was surprised to see how much more like the old Leah she looked. Apart from her hair. She hadn't bothered with straighteners for months, and she certainly hadn't thought to bring them here, with Jaco breathing down her neck as she had been bullied into packing her belongings.

Releasing the band that held her ponytail, she shook her head so that the loose curls

fell over her shoulders. Then, picking up her brush, she set about taming them as best she could, vigorously brushing until her hair shone.

Finally ready, she stood up, firmly pulling down the hem of the halter-neck minidress she was wearing. She had very little in the way of clothes here—hardly surprising, considering the circumstances. This emerald-green number was the only thing she had that even approached 'smart', and it seemed a whole lot snugger now than it had when she had worn it pre-Gabriel—before her life had been turned upside down.

Smoothing the lightweight jersey fabric over her bottom and across her bust, she wondered if maybe it was too revealing. Oh, what the hell? Picking up the baby monitor, Leah peeped into the crib one last time to check that Gabriel was sound asleep, and headed for the living room. What difference did it make anyway? Jaco would probably barely notice what she had on. They were having a meal together this evening to talk about the future, about how they could make it work with the three of them. It was most definitely *not* about anything else.

Leah could hardly believe she was contemplating *any* sort of future with Jaco in it, but

what choice did she have? He was Gabriel's father, after all, and such was his determination, his wealth and influence, she strongly suspected that to fight against him would prove to be futile. Worse than futile. If she continued to struggle she would just be causing herself more pain.

So when Jaco had suggested that they sit down for a meal together and talk things through, and had said that he would cook, she had fought against her natural instinct to tell him what he could do with his cooking and reluctantly agreed instead. Her only hope was that she could make him see sense—see that the three of them living together could never, *ever* work.

The open-plan living area was empty when Leah walked in, the wide glass doors open so that a gentle breeze stirred the air. Ignoring the strip of dark blue water bisecting the room, she moved to the doorway, letting her shoulders drop for a minute as she took in the expansive view of the sea and the sky, bathed in soft evening light. Cicadas chirped in the ancient olive trees as she breathed in the scent of jasmine and lavender, the slight tang of sea spray carried in on the breeze.

It occurred to Leah that on paper this place was as close to paradise as you were ever

likely to get. But having to share paradise with the pervasive influence of a dark and brooding Jaco Valentino meant it felt more as if she had dropped through the burning doors of hell.

A sound to her left made her turn her head, and Jaco appeared from the steps that led down to the terraced garden. Wearing black jeans and a white tee shirt, he looked relaxed and bronzed and as effortlessly handsome as ever. He stopped when he saw her, pushing his sunglasses up onto his head, and his eyes travelled rapidly over Leah's body, leaving a blazing trail in their wake.

'You look…' His hesitation only set Leah's heart thumping harder. *'Molto bella.'*

'Thanks.' She couldn't meet his eye. She didn't want his smooth, well-worn compliments. Instead she glanced at the small bunch of herbs in his hand. 'What's that?'

'Oregano.' He advanced towards her. 'It grows wild around here.' He crushed some of the leaves between his fingers and held them in the palm of his hand. 'Here—smell that.'

Leah did as she was told, inhaling deeply, closing her eyes to block out his nearness. She opened them again to see Jaco staring intently at her. For a moment he didn't move. Seconds passed.

'Right, well…' Finally Jaco broke the silence, his throat sounding parched. 'I guess I'd better get on with the cooking.'

'Anything I can do to help?' She badly needed to do something practical—anything to take her mind off the sexual tension that was swirling around them like an impending storm.

'No, no, it's all under control.'

Of course it was. When *wasn't* every aspect of Jaco's life under control?

As Leah watched his retreating back every nerve in her body still hummed from that small exchange. From the way he had looked at her, the hunger in his eyes. It was the same hunger that had been there from the start—from their very first meeting.

Walking unsteadily into the living room, Leah seated herself at the end of the long glass dining table, where Jaco had set two places. How come she still felt that pull? That physical tug that had her heart racing, her breasts tingling, her whole body craving him? How could she still want him so badly after the way he had treated her? Now that she knew the kind of man he really was? But the fact was she did. And, unless she was very much mistaken, he felt it too.

Jaco came back into the room, holding an

ice bucket to his chest. Leah watched as he took out a bottle, untwisting the wire from around the cork and expertly popping it free. Quickly filling two glass flutes, he handed one to her before seating himself opposite.

'Try this.' His eyes didn't leave her face. 'I would like your opinion.'

'It's from Capezzana?' Leah took the glass from him, glad of the distraction.

Jaco nodded. '*Sí*, it's the first sparkling wine we have produced. A blend of chardonnay and *pino nero* grapes, using the traditional *metodo classico*.'

Leah took a sip and felt the creamy bubbles slide down her throat. 'It's delicious.' She took another sip, savouring the taste in her mouth for a moment before swallowing. 'Hints of vanilla and lemon…dry, but aromatic.'

A smile quirked the corner of Jaco's mouth. 'I see I have taught you well.'

Suddenly self-conscious, Leah looked away. 'Have you started marketing it yet?'

'No, not yet.' Jaco took a healthy sip of the wine before returning his all-seeing gaze to her face. 'I lost my marketing manager a year ago and haven't managed to replace her yet.'

Leah's spine stiffened. 'I'm sure there are plenty of people who would love to do that job.'

'Maybe. But no one as good as you, Leah.'

'I didn't do anything special.'

'I think we both know that's not true. I would say you were very special.'

Leah looked down, cursing the flush that was creeping over her cheeks.

'You were a great marketing manager and you know it,' Jaco continued dryly. 'Which is why I want you to get involved again.'

Leah gaped at him in surprise. 'You are offering me a job?'

'No, not a job.'

'Good.' She let out a derisive huff. 'Then that will save me having to turn you down.'

A pulse twitched in Jaco's cheek and he took a breath, casting his eyes down as he found the control to continue.

'I am not offering you a job...' he took another swallow of wine, his Adam's apple moving in his throat '...but a way of life. A future. Somewhere for you and Gabriel to settle, put down roots. I would like you to have an active role in the running of the vineyard.'

He raised his eyes and suddenly Leah could see just how much this meant to him reflected in his midnight gaze. Not that that offered her any sort of comfort—far from it. Instead she felt the ties that bound them together pulling tighter all the time, wrapping around her, re-

stricting her limbs and compressing her chest, squeezing the air out of her.

'You mean you want to put us to work?' It was a sulky reply, designed to cover up her deep unease. 'Perhaps you would like Gabriel to crush the grapes for you, or maybe crawl under the vines to reach the low-hanging fruit?'

'It's a thought.'

Her sarcasm backfired spectacularly when Jaco's sensuous smile arrowed straight to her wounded heart.

'It is a family business after all.'

A family business. Leah gazed at him from beneath lowered lashes. She knew exactly what family meant to proud Sicilians like Jaco. She knew she had no chance of ever fighting against its vice-like hold.

She took another sip of wine, letting it slide down her throat, hoping to cool the heat of anxiety that was starting to raise her core temperature.

The fact that Jaco was determined she and Gabriel should make Capezzana their home, when no doubt he had countless properties all over the world, felt ominously significant. The Capezzana estate had been in his family for generations—his birth parents had owned it before the tragic accident that had taken

their lives. She remembered being told by the estate workers that Jaco had bought it back a few years ago, restoring the *palazzo* and the neglected vineyard as a mark of respect to them. It didn't take much imagination to work out Jaco's intentions.

'So, did you grow up at Capezzana?' She asked the question lightly, in the way a hostage might try to engage her captor in conversation.

'Yes.' Jaco's reply was quick, brusque. 'Until I was five.'

'That was when your parents died?'

'Sí.'

'And it means a lot to you?'

'Yes, it does.' Defensive now, he stared coldly back at her. 'Capezzana is the only property I own with any family history. It is fitting that my son should grow up there.'

There it was—all her worst fears confirmed, spoken from the perfectly formed lips of the man himself. She had absolutely no ammunition against this sort of history. This sort of control.

'And my family count for nothing, I suppose?' Still she wriggled on the hook.

'Your sister and your nephew have already made their home in Sicily. Your father is welcome to visit any time he chooses.' His jaw

flexed with determination. 'Obviously you can visit your homeland as often as you like. But Gabriel's home will be at Capezzana.'

'And when, exactly, did *you* get to make all the rules?'

'Fighting this is futile, Leah. You might just as well accept that.'

With infuriating calmness, he pushed back his chair and got to his feet. Leah could only gawp with surprise as he turned away and started towards the kitchen.

'So…' He addressed her over his arrogantly angled shoulder. 'How do you like your steak?'

So that was it, was it? Decided?

Jaco's idea of talking things through, working things out, had been nothing more than an excuse for him to deliver his dictate—tell her exactly what was going to happen?

Humming with impotent fury, Leah watched his retreating figure. Then, slamming down her wine glass, she followed him into the sleek kitchen, positioning herself behind him with her hands on her hips. Just to fire her up even more, Jaco totally ignored her, busying himself putting the griddle pan on the hob, then stripping the oregano leaves into the mortar and using the pestle to grind them into a paste with garlic and olive oil.

Through a haze of red mist, Leah dimly acknowledged that she'd had no idea he could cook. But then she'd had no idea about anything when it came to Jaco Valentino.

Picking up the first of two steaks, he spread the mixture on both sides and laid it on the pan, where it sizzled temptingly.

'Medium okay for you?' He started to spread the second steak. 'I like mine pretty rare, but I know that's not to everyone's taste.'

'You mean I get a choice?' Leah growled at him. 'You seem so hell-bent on controlling my life, I'm surprised that doesn't include what I put in my mouth.'

She had been aiming for barbed sarcasm, but somehow her innocent words had come out all wrong and a flush rapidly spread over her cheeks. And when Jaco slowly turned to face her, his deliberately provocative gaze seemed to suck all the oxygen from the room.

'I wouldn't dream of dictating what you put in your mouth.' His voice was as rich as dark chocolate, as smooth as silk. 'Though I do remember being on very intimate terms with it.'

Leah's flush turned even more violent as she desperately searched for some sort of clever retort—any retort at all, in fact.

'And very pleasurable it was too…'

Too late. Before she could do so much as

pull in a gasp of air Jaco had seized the moment, taking her breath along with it.

He made his move. Drifting his fingertips along her jawline, curling his hand around the side of her neck, sliding aside the curtain of hair and firmly drawing her to him. Leah's heart thundered inside her. She knew she should push him away, but with his thumb rhythmically stroking her jaw, the heat of his palm on her neck, she first had to fight the tide of pleasure. And when Jaco lowered his head, his breath hot against her cheek, Leah felt her lips tingle, swelling with blood, parting, silently begging to be kissed.

The kiss, when it came, was hot and fierce and punishing. With the fingers of both hands threading through her hair, Jaco pinned her body against his, using his mouth like a weapon of destruction—the destruction of her willpower, her resolve, any sense of reason.

Surge after surge of frantic sensation crashed over her as Jaco's mouth performed its erotic onslaught, his tongue tangling with hers, wet and sweet, his lips working their wicked magic and his teeth occasionally nipping at the softness of her lower lip in a blatant display of dominance and control.

His hands left her face, rapidly moving

over her bare shoulders and down her back, smoothing over the curve of her buttocks, where they stopped. His fingers branded her skin beneath the tight fabric of her dress before they clenched firmly, pulling her to him, the swell of his arousal pressing against her stomach, sending her into a spiral of deep and desperate longing.

Stumbling forward, Jaco took Leah with him, their bodies a tangle of limbs and flesh and gasping breath until Leah felt her back pressing against the wall. Jaco's hands went to the tops of her arms and his head dipped to kiss her again, his chest heaving.

'*Dio*, Leah.' His voice was thick with desire. 'What is it with you? Why do you do this to me?'

Leah could ask the same question of him. Actually, she couldn't, having totally lost the power of speech along with all her other faculties.

Towering over her, exuding a dark, masculine power all his own, Jaco found the hem of her dress and slipped his hand tantalisingly beneath, sliding upwards between her inner thighs, making Leah tremble with delicious longing until he reached her panties, where his fingers began to trace the outline of the lacy fabric with a featherlight touch.

Leah held herself very still, silently willing him to carry on, at the same time knowing that she really, *really* shouldn't want him to. That this was madness.

His fingers followed the line of her panties to where the swollen nub of her throbbed with forbidden need. She desperately wanted him to go further, to slip underneath and work his magic in a way that she knew only he could. Only he *ever* could.

She moaned softly, arching her hips so that his hand pressed more firmly against her, leaving him in no doubt about what she wanted and how badly she wanted it. Not that she needed to spell it out. She had never had any defence against Jaco's power, against the sheer sexual magnetism of him, and well he knew it.

He responded with a primal grunt of satisfaction or need or both. Leah no longer had the capability to work it out. It didn't matter anyway. His fingers started to slide beneath her panties and Leah closed her eyes.

Only to snap them open as a piercing shriek echoed around the room, blasting her eardrums.

'Merda!'

Cursing violently, Jaco pulled away and marched over to the hob. The burning steak had set off the smoke alarm. Picking up the

handle of the pan, he let out a violent Sicilian curse, flinging the pan to the floor.

'Sanguinoso inferno!'

The swearing continued, and Leah fought to suppress a smile as he leapt up onto the island work station, stretching to reach the alarm on the ceiling and frantically pressing buttons until finally the terrible noise stopped. Then he paused, placing his hands on his hips, his gaze travelling from the mess on the floor to where Leah still stood by the wall, her clothes now pulled back into place.

'You did say charred, right?'

Leah burst out laughing. She couldn't help it. 'Come here.' She walked towards him. 'Let me see that hand.'

'It's nothing.' Towering over her like a colossus, feet apart, hands on hips, Jaco gazed down at her, clearly in no hurry to relinquish his position of great height.

'Come on.' Leah beckoned to him, and after a moment's pause Jaco jumped down beside her, obediently holding out his palm.

Leah took his hand in hers, turning it to catch the light. A red patch was forming on the lower pads of his fingers.

'You need to run it under cold water.' Before he had the chance to object she reached across his body, taking his hand with her, and

turned on the tap, holding his fingers under the running water.

Jaco gave her a sideways glance. ‘You make a good nurse.’ Leah removed her hand, but when Jaco did the same she shoved his back under the tap. ‘Bossy, but sexy with it.’

‘Then do as you’re told and keep your hand under that water while I clear up this mess.’

She turned away, intent on distracting herself from Jaco’s deliberate teasing. For this was a glimpse of the old Jaco—the one she’d thought she had known. Cheeky, sexy, fun to be around. It was the first time she had seen it in the whole time they had been on the island.

‘Leave it, Leah.’ He turned off the tap and caught hold of her shoulder.

‘Well, someone is going to have to—’

‘I said leave it.’ Suddenly serious again, he moved his hand to the small of her back, pulling her against him again. ‘We have unfinished business to attend to.’

‘Jaco… I…’

But suddenly his mouth was on hers again, hot and raw and punishing, stealing all reason. And when he broke the kiss to sweep her up into his arms Leah held on tight, burying her face in his collarbone, pressing her nose into the hollow at the base of his throat so that she could inhale his unique exotic scent.

And she knew right there and then that she was totally lost.

After carrying her through to the living room Jaco set her down, plunging his fingers through her hair and capturing her mouth again. Leah slid her arms down the broad width of his back, feeling the muscles flex and buck beneath her touch. Releasing her for a second, Jaco crossed his arms over his chest and, feeling for the bottom of his tee shirt, roughly pulled it over his head and cast it aside.

Leah took a moment to savour the image of his physique in the dying light of the room: the width of his shoulders, the smooth curve of his rock-hard pecs, the tight, dark nipples, the pronounced six-pack of a man who was no stranger to a workout, the line of dark hair descending into his low-slung jeans. He really was perfection personified.

Leah raised her hands to smooth his deliciously ruffled hair, but Jaco took hold of her wrists, his eyes glittering with raw, animal desire.

'Bed.'

The single word was uttered with all the heavy, dark promise of what was to come. Threading his fingers through hers, he pulled her against him and together they stumbled a

couple of steps across the living room, their bodies pressed together, their feet tripping each other up, until they gave up completely and came to a standstill with the strip of glass floor beneath their feet, the water glinting darkly.

With his eyes focussed solely on her face, Jaco caught the hem of Leah's dress and tugged it up to her waist. His hands moved to caress her bottom through her panties, and he made a deep groaning noise against her throat as he kissed her again.

Leah felt for the buttons of his jeans with trembling fingers, drawing in a sharp breath at the way they strained against the might of the hot, hard column of flesh beneath. She fumbled to release the first couple of buttons but, impatient, Jaco took over, ripping them open with a sharp tug, then pulling down his jeans and his boxers with them, until he was gloriously stark naked.

Drawing her to him again, he slid his hot hands over the tops of her thighs before looping his fingers through the flimsy fabric of her panties and sliding them down her legs, kneeling at her feet and lifting first one and then the other so he could cast the lace aside.

Leah stared down at him, at the dark curls on his head, the tanned skin of the bunched

muscles of his back and shoulders, gazing at the sheer power and pleasure there, waiting to be unleashed.

And then he was standing again, pulling her to him, his arms around her back, pressing the full length of his naked body against her, moving her backwards to the white leather sofa where they fell down together. Leah found herself on top of Jaco as their legs wound around each other, their mouths crushing, melding, their breathing coming in hot, hard pants, merging until it was impossible to know whose breath was whose, until they were one and the same.

With her dress still bunched up around her waist, Leah freed her arms to try and peel it over her head, but a growl from Jaco stopped her and he brought her back down, lifting her hips to position himself perfectly beneath her. And then, after an agonising split second of a pause, he thrust, plunging the whole, hot, hard, silky length of himself inside her.

Leah gasped with shock and pleasure. The sheer size of him, the intensely intimate sensation making her sink her nails into his bare flesh. It had been such a long time she had almost forgotten the power of this—the extraordinary feeling of profound desire coupled with deep and urgent need.

And yet as Jaco started to move inside her, picking up a primal, erotic rhythm, it felt so blissfully, orgasmically *right*—as if her whole body had been dormant until this moment, frozen, sleeping, waiting to be awoken by this handsome prince. She could already feel the tremor of an orgasm starting to tingle inside her, rapidly building up to a tidal wave of strength until she started to shake with the effort of containing it, and she knew she wouldn't be able to hang on much longer.

'Not yet.'

With a guttural moan Jaco gripped her hips more tightly, his fingers digging into her flesh as he used the span of his hands to steady her so that he could thrust harder, even more deeply. His eyes flickered beneath half-closed lids, and as Leah gazed down at him she could see that he was battling to hold back his own release—that even now, even in the throes of such carnal lust, he had to be in control, commanding that she did as she was told, that neither of them would come until he gave his permission.

Well, she would see about that. Pushing her hands against his chest, which was slicked with sweat, Leah jerked her torso upright, arching her back and throwing back her head, deepening the glorious sensation

of his thrusts still further. He could do this to her—he could make her feel like no other man ever could—but he couldn't control her response.

And then she let herself go. Freely giving herself over to her orgasm, she let it take her wherever it wanted to, over the edge of the cliff and into free fall, her body jerking and writhing as sensation after sensation passed through her. She lifted her chin to the ceiling, her hair cascading down her back as she bucked and trembled. Somewhere in the midst of her intense euphoria she became aware that Jaco had also given way to his own release. And that each was gasping the other's name.

CHAPTER SEVEN

JACO GAZED UP at Leah through narrowed eyes as he waited for his heart rate to steady, for his breathing to return to something like normal. She was still sitting astride him, with her head thrown back and her hands loosening on his chest muscles, and he followed the pale column of her throat, the V of her jawline shadowed in the fading light. So beautiful.

He had been fantasising about making love to her ever since they had been on this island. No, for far longer than that if he was being truthful—ever since that last time, the night that his son had been conceived.

Over the past year he had tried to convince himself that she meant nothing to him, that he was over Leah McDonald. Entirely unaccustomed to being dumped, he had taken her rejection at face value, told himself it was her loss. But deep down he knew it wasn't just his pride that had taken a knock, that it was more

than just a slap in the face. The sting of a slap quickly faded, but the burn of Leah's rebuff had stayed with him. More than that, it had grown, gnawing away at him until the only way to rid himself of the canker had been to take her again. To prove to himself, *and to her*, that he had the power to recreate the magic they had shared. That he could make her scream his name again.

The fact that he, too, had lost control, that somehow her name had escaped his lips at the moment of orgasm, was something he preferred not to dwell on.

Leah's head came up, and the glazed look of euphoria was quickly dispelled by a flash of something like confusion in her eyes.

The moment was over, as Jaco had known it would be—which was a pity. He could happily have taken her again. The sight of her swollen lips, her flushed cheeks and the tousled hair that she was now forcibly tucking behind her ears, was already threatening to harden him again inside her.

Levering herself off him, Leah stood unsteadily on the floor, pulling down her dress and looking around her with a slightly dazed expression, as if she wasn't sure what to do now. Jaco swung his legs off the sofa and positioned himself in front of her, his feet apart,

his arms folded over his chest. He watched as she tilted her chin, forcing herself to meet his gaze—a gaze that he was not prepared to spare her.

A surge of anger swept through him. Why did she find it so hard to make eye contact? Why could she hardly bring herself to look at him? They had done nothing wrong. As far as he knew, sex between single consenting adults was perfectly legal—even in the infuriatingly skewed world of Leah McDonald.

He certainly had no intention of apologising for what had just happened. He didn't regret it. But as he stared at the hurt and anguish etched across her face he knew without a shred of doubt that she did.

Well, so be it. That was *her* problem.

With a silent growl of frustration, Jaco turned away to retrieve his jeans from where he had flung them across the floor. Without bothering with his boxers, he tugged them on, staring out at the darkening sky through the open glass doors as he buttoned up the fly. He could feel Leah's eyes on him as surely as if he could see her, and that only increased his bitter frustration.

Oh, yeah, *now* she could look at him. Now he had his back to her. No doubt she was coming up with all sorts of excuses in that

pretty little head of hers to justify her actions. No doubt he was going to be painted as the bad guy. No doubt it had all been *his* fault.

It seemed that Leah had the capacity to twist the truth to suit her purposes, to make herself the victim. Though why she should want to do that he had no idea. Unless maybe it was a guilty conscience for keeping Gabriel's existence a secret.

But right now he didn't have the patience to try and work it out. If they were going to live together—and for the sake of his son Jaco was going to make damned sure they did—they were going to have to find some way to break through this protective wall Leah had erected around herself. A way that didn't involve sex. Because that seemed to be the only thing they did right. *Too* right.

Despite everything, Jaco knew that he would have Leah in his bed every night if he had his way—that he would never tire of her luscious body and the way she gave it so freely, her soft moans of arousal, the wild shrieks of ecstasy. He wanted her as he had never wanted any other woman, and right now, with Leah's self-righteous eyes boring into his back, that didn't feel good. It felt like a weakness. One that he had to conquer.

Jamming his hands into his jeans pockets,

he turned around, deliberately ignoring Leah, who appeared to be still rooted to the spot by her own antipathy.

'I'm going to have another go at making something to eat.' He strode past her, heading for the kitchen. 'Do you want to join me?'

'No.'

Her reply was as emphatic as he had known it would be.

'I'm… I'm going to take a shower.'

'As you wish.'

He certainly wasn't going to try and persuade her. She could take all the showers she wanted—run the water to scalding hot, scrub her skin until it was red and raw—but it wouldn't make any difference. It still wouldn't erase what they had just done. Leah could fight it all she liked, but the fact was they hungered for each other, they *burned* for one another. And there wasn't a damned thing either of them could do about it.

Leah stared at the broad expanse of Jaco's bare back as he marched towards the kitchen, her shoulders finally sagging as she let out a shuddering breath.

Well done, Leah. Of all the things she really, *really* shouldn't have done, having wild, passionate sex with Jaco on the sofa was right

up there. Hadn't she been telling herself since day one on this island that she had to be on her guard against this happening? That despite everything she knew about Jaco—or, more importantly, *didn't* know—he still had a hold over her that she couldn't break.

She was all too aware that he could set her on fire with a flash of those brown eyes. That she still fell apart under his touch. Which was why she should never have agreed to have supper with him. She should never have put herself in such a vulnerable position when she had absolutely no protection against this man.

Furious with herself, she cast about, finding where her knickers had been discarded and untwisting the flimsy fabric, pulling them back on. And that was when she saw it. A mobile phone—Jaco's mobile phone. Lying under a low table in front of the window where it must have fallen out of Jaco's jeans when he'd hurled them across the floor.

Cautiously, Leah made her way towards it. She could hear Jaco banging about in the kitchen, clattering pans in a way that suggested he wasn't any happier about what they had just done than she was. Bending down, she reached under the table, closing her hand over the phone and holding it against her chest

as she stood up, casting a furtive look over her shoulder in the direction of the kitchen.

This was it—her chance to get off this island, for her and Gabriel to escape. With her heart thudding, she brought the screen to life. It was locked, of course, but there was an emergency button at the bottom. She touched it with a trembling finger, pressing the phone to her ear so hard it hurt and moving to the corner of the room, so that she had the best chance of making herself heard whilst still listening out for Jaco.

The phone was answered immediately. 'Hi, yes—*sí*. I need the police—*polizia*. Right away...*pronto*.'

The woman at the other end of the phone replied in rapid Italian and Leah felt her heart sink. Oh, God, why had she never learnt the language properly?

'English. *Inglese*,' she tried desperately. 'Do you speak English?'

To Leah's intense relief, the woman calmly replied that she did.

'Oh, thank you!' she breathed into the phone. 'You must come quickly. I have been kidnapped. Me and my baby son. You have to come and rescue us.'

The words tumbled out in a hoarse, barely coherent whisper.

'I don't know exactly where we are, but it's a private island off the coast of Sicily, somewhere to the north. It is owned by Jaco Valentino. He used to be called Garalino. He has been keeping us here for nearly two weeks and he's taken away my phone and… *Yes*, you have to believe me… My name? It's Leah McDonald… No, I can't speak up, because he is here and he might come in at any moment… M-C-D-O-N-A-L-D… Yes, that's right. Leah. L-E-A-H… No, no—whatever you do, don't ring back on this number, because it is *his* phone… I don't *have* a contact number—I told you, he's taken my phone. You have to come and find us right away… No, I'm not in any imminent danger as such… No, he's not physically violent. But what I'm saying is the truth! Please… *Listen* to me… Oh, God, he's coming back. I have to go.'

Rapidly ending the call as she heard Jaco approaching, Leah hurried to slide the phone back under the table, where she had found it, straightening up and rearranging her features just in time as he walked in.

'Still here?' All mocking arrogance, Jaco cast his eyes around the room.

For all his nonchalance, Leah knew exactly what he was looking for. Bending down, he picked up his tee shirt and Leah saw his

eyes alight on the phone. She watched as he strolled over to retrieve it before jamming it into the back pocket of his jeans.

Phew, she had got away with it! Now all she had to do was wait to be rescued. She didn't know how or when, but surely someone would come to her aid?

'Yes, I'm still here.' Emboldened by what she had just managed to do, Leah gave him a defiant pout. 'For the time being, anyway.'

Jaco narrowed his eyes, studying her far more closely than she had intended. Or wanted. Why on earth had she said that? She needed to be so much more careful around this man.

'I mean, I'm going to have that shower now.' Still she hesitated, though she didn't know why.

'Fine.' Jaco gave her a look of disdain, designed to show her how little he cared. 'Be my guest.'

Leah turned to go, but then, with fire still coursing through her veins, she swung back. 'But I'm *not* your guest, am I?' She shot him a combative stare. 'I am your prisoner.'

'Call it what you like.'

Jaco folded his arms across his bare chest. Why couldn't he put some clothes on? Why was he still taunting her?

'But I will say that for someone who is being kept here against her will you have been remarkably accommodating.' His eyes glittered with scorn. 'I don't seem to recall you complaining about being held captive just now. Quite the reverse, in fact.'

Leah felt the blood ringing in her ears. 'Why, you arrogant son of a—' Hurling herself towards him, she raised her hand, wanting nothing more than to wipe that smug, supercilious sneer off his supremely self-satisfied face with a hard slap.

But Jaco caught her wrist with the ease of a man who had probably done it several times before, bringing it down to his chest and holding it firmly in his grip.

'Temper, temper.' He stared calmly down at her, a maddening smirk playing on his lips. 'You really need to try and control these outbursts, you know.'

Leah growled with anger, tugging to try and free herself.

'Or maybe it's some sort of Scottish thing—flying off the handle at the slightest thing.'

The fury was now flowing through her like a river of molten metal. If it wasn't enough insulting her—he was now disrespecting her whole country.

'Something to do with your Celtic blood... all that red hair?'

'Or maybe it's to do with the fact that you are a lying, cheating, two-timing bastard!'

Silence fell around them like a wall of lead.

'I beg your pardon?' Jaco dropped her wrist as if were white-hot. 'What did you just call me?'

'A lying, cheating, two-timing bastard.' Leah repeated the words with as much authority as she could drag up when he was looking at her with the coldly murderous stare of a trained assassin. 'Because that is what you are.'

Jaco's eyes narrowed, glinting like steel. He raised his hand to his neck, as if to stop the words from forming in his throat as he continued to stare at her, making no sound apart from the exhalation of breath from his flared nostrils.

Leah shifted her weight from one foot to the other. She needed to hold herself steady, to stop the tremor that was starting to shake her knees, making her hands tremble. He was such a formidable presence, so darkly, intensely forceful, that when he unleashed this sort of quiet assault it was almost impossible not to be slain by the power of it.

But she refused to be slain. She would

stand up to him because she had done nothing wrong. She had only spoken the truth.

'So let me get this straight.' With soft but deadly assurance Jaco reached out, curling his hand around the back of Leah's head and tilting it upwards so that she had no escape from his gaze in the dying light. 'You are accusing me of cheating?'

'Yes.' Leah swallowed hard. 'Yes, I am.'

'And tell me…' His voice was terrifyingly calm, his breath hot on her upturned face. 'Just what right do you have to call into question anything I may or may not have done in the last twelve months?'

'So you don't deny it, then?' Leah persisted, despite the profound pain coursing through her.

'I have no intention of confirming or denying anything to you.' He released her head as if he no longer wanted to touch her, his voice a contemptuous sneer. 'May I remind you that *you* were the one who walked out on me? What I have done in the intervening time, who I have slept with, is none of your damned business.'

'I'm not talking about the *intervening* time.' Leah struggled to pull out the dagger in her heart, to ignore the searing agony of imagining him with another woman, taking her in

his arms, making love to her. 'I am talking about when we were together.'

'When we were *together*?'

Twisting the blade still deeper, Jaco repeated the word as if it had been far too long ago—or, worse still, too pifflingly insignificant—for him to even remember. Or maybe he had never considered them to be an item.

'Yes.'

It took all her reserves of courage and bravado to say the word, when every fibre of her being wanted to scream and shout and beat her fists against his callous, heartless, stony chest. To rage that something that had meant everything to her could have meant so little to him.

'You think I was cheating on you *then*?'

He looked genuinely baffled. A great performance.

Leah glared back. If he was going to try and lie his way out of this she was going to hate him even more.

'I don't think—I *know*. You were cheating on both of us.'

Jaco's dark brows knotted. He was looking at her as if she had completely lost it. 'I have absolutely no idea what you are talking about, Leah. Where is that crazy brain of yours taking you?'

'Crazy, eh?' Leah hurled back. 'I'm sure that would suit you just fine, wouldn't it? To make out that I'm *crazy* because I've found out what you have been up to. Because I know your shameful secret.'

Suddenly he was deadly still, poised like a cobra about to strike. 'And what, *exactly*, do you mean by that?'

Ah, yes, *now* she had got his attention.

'I *know*, Jaco.' She fixed him with a piercing stare. 'I know about Francesca!'

There—she had said it. Spilt the poison that had been eating her up inside for so long.

There was a shocked beat of silence before Jaco finally spoke.

'Francesca?'

Her name whispered across his lips in a way that made Leah's heart constrict with pain. The colour had drained from his face; shock stiffening his spine. He looked completely stunned, horrified—almost felled by this appalling disclosure.

But if Leah had thought she would get any satisfaction from his torment, any sense of revenge, she had been sorely mistaken. Jaco's extreme reaction only served to demonstrate just how much this woman meant to him. It was written all over his horrified face.

'How the *hell* do you know about Francesca?' The question was spat from his lips.

So there was to be no denial, no excuse.

'It doesn't matter how I know.' Leah broke eye contact, looking down and twisting her clasped hands in front of her. Hearing him say the name of his lover out loud felt unbelievably painful—as if he was ripping open a wound that hadn't even begun to heal. 'The point is that I do.'

'Oh, trust me, it matters a great deal.' He grasped hold of her shoulders, forcing her to look at him again. 'Tell me, Leah. Tell me right now how you know.'

'Very well.' His wide-eyed urgency was starting to frighten her. Who on earth was this wild, intimidating stranger, barely holding on to his control? But she had nothing to lose by telling him everything now. 'I saw you…the two of you…having a *very* cosy video conversation.'

'What? When?'

She could see him racking his brains.

'That last evening at Capezzana?' Releasing one shoulder, Jaco forcefully raked a hand through his hair as realisation started to dawn. 'Before you threw in your job the next day and took off?'

Leah silently raised her eyebrows. It was all the acknowledgment he was getting.

'*Dio*, Leah.' Anguish etched his face before determination set in again. 'And what have you done with this information?'

What sort of a question was that?

Leah fought to hold herself steady. 'I would have thought that was obvious. I got the hell out. Once I'd realised the sort of man you really are I wanted nothing more to do with you. I still don't.'

'And who else have you told about Francesca?'

'No one.'

'Harper—your sister—have you told her?'

'No, I've already said I haven't told anyone.'

What was this? Some sort of inquisition? How come he was treating her as if she was the one who had committed the crime?

'Your sordid little secret is safe with me.'

He turned his face away, cursing in his native tongue before swinging back to look at her.

'So let me get this straight.'

She felt as if his dark eyes could bore holes into her soul.

'You thought I was having an affair with Francesca and that was the reason you left?'

'Got it in one.'

'Even though you knew you were pregnant?'

'*Especially* because I knew I was pregnant.' Leah glared at him with shaky defiance. 'I would far rather raise my child alone than subject him to a father who clearly has no morals, no sense of decency.'

'*Dannazione*, Leah,' he growled in bitter frustration. 'You hurl accusations at me, you walk out of my life and you deny me the knowledge that I have a son. And yet it never occurred to you to *ask* me about Francesca? About who she actually is?'

'No, funnily enough, it didn't.' Leah refused to be cowed. 'In the same way as it obviously never occurred to *you* to mention her to me.'

'Well, let me tell you right now: my relationship with Francesca is not what you think.'

'No?'

Relationship in the present tense.

The knowledge that it was still going on brought a new wave of pain, easily breaching the barriers of self-defence that she had worked so hard to construct. So this Francesca woman wasn't just a brief fling—one of any number of casual lovers that Jaco

might have taken up with, then dropped. This woman was still around. This woman meant something. It was written all over his glowering face.

Leah sucked in a breath, her hands shaking slightly as she pushed her hair away from her face. 'So, please, do tell—what exactly *is* your relationship with the lovely Francesca?' She deliberately piled on the sarcasm to disguise her pain.

There was a second's silence, a beat of hesitation. Leah watched as Jaco bit down on his lip, registering the taut set of his jaw, the play of muscles beneath his skin as he figured out what he was going to say.

Finally he spoke. 'Francesca is my sister.'

Leah felt her shoulders sag with the weight of the pathetic lie. Was that it? Was that really the best he could come up with?

'Yeah, right.' She gave a humourless laugh. 'Unfortunately for you, Jaco, I know your background. One birth sibling, male, adopted with you into a family with two older siblings, also male. You can see I have done my research.'

'Your research has failed to uncover one important fact.' He hesitated again, as if he could hardly bring himself to say the words. 'Because this is something that no one knows.

My birth brother, Francesco, is now my birth sister—Francesca.'

'What…?' Leah's mouth fell open. 'You mean…?'

'Yes, Leah, exactly that. She has had gender reassignment surgery.'

Leah gazed at him in stunned astonishment, realisation sinking in with every second that ticked by. Now she thought about it, there *had* been a resemblance between the face she had seen on the computer screen and Jaco's own. Something about the tilt of the head, the intensity of those dark brown eyes…

'But why all the secrecy?' She gulped the question. 'I mean, why does nobody know the truth?'

'Because there are people who would use that information against her. People who would like to hurt her.'

'But who? *What* people?'

'You don't need to concern yourself with that.'

Leah growled with frustration. 'But she can't hide herself away—live in secret for the rest of her life. Not after everything she must have already gone through.'

'She won't have to. Not for much longer.'

She could hear the determination in his

voice, see the emotion, the pride. And suddenly she knew without a shred of doubt that everything he said was true.

Oh, God.

The realisation drained the blood from her head and the room started to do a giddy spin. In one way it felt as if the iron fist around her poor crushed heart had finally loosened its grip, but in another she realised now just what she had done—accused Jaco of a crime he hadn't committed and kept from him the knowledge that he had a son.

'Are you okay?'

She was dimly aware that Jaco was speaking to her. There was concern in his voice now, replacing the grim authority of before.

'Leah?' He moved her hair aside so that he could see her better.

'Yes.' Leah attempted a small laugh. 'Yes, of course.'

'You look like you need to sit down.'

Without waiting for her assent, he moved her over to the sofa. The same sofa that had so recently seen them cavorting in the throcs of reckless passion. Turning her to face him, gently now, he looked deep into her eyes, and the intensity of his ebony gaze, the surprising compassion held there, did nothing to help regulate her breathing.

'You are very pale.' He brushed a gentle finger along the length of her lips. 'Are you sure you're okay?'

'Yes, honestly, I'm fine.' Leah sat up a little straighter, making a supreme effort to appear normal. 'But I might just get a glass of water...'

'Stay there.' Jaco placed a firm hand on her thigh. 'I'll get it.'

Leah drew in a much-needed breath as she watched him stride towards the kitchen. *Francesca was his sister!* That changed everything—but then again it changed nothing. Maybe it explained why Jaco had been so furious with her, but not why he had kidnapped her and Gabriel. Why he was keeping them prisoner.

But she had no time to order her scattered thoughts before Jaco reappeared, handing her a glass of water and sitting himself down beside her.

She took a sip, realising how much her hand was shaking from the way the water rippled across the surface.

'So...' Jaco edged closer. '*"A lying, cheating, two-timing bastard."* That's what you think of me, is it?'

'No... I mean that's what I thought...' Leah swallowed another shaky gulp.

'Nice to know you have such a high opinion of me, Leah.'

He took the glass from her hand and set it down on the table, then turned her to face him so that she couldn't miss the dark mockery in his gaze.

'Well, what was I supposed to think?'

Leah angled her head away, but Jaco caught hold of her chin and turned her to face him again. He was clearly going to spare her no mercy.

'Don't.'

'Don't what?' With the compelling force of Jaco's glittering gaze stealing all reason, Leah had no idea about anything any more.

'Don't think.'

Jaco helpfully supplied her with the answer, tracing her jawline with a feather-light finger that rippled a slide of sensation through her senses.

'Thinking only gets you into trouble. Now is the time to *show* me how sorry you are.'

'Who says I'm sorry?'

The arrogance of this man was astounding. As was the sudden lack of air in the room, and the sweeping sexual current that was dragging her under, making it impossible to breathe.

'*I* do, Leah.' His voice was a low, sexy

drawl, and a feral glow was burning in his eyes. 'I think you are very sorry indeed. But if you are not able to voice your apology I will have to find another way to drag it out of you.'

His lowered his head until it was just inches from her upturned face. The hot beat of his breath scorched her cheeks.

'And I have no say in the matter?'

'Uh-uh—no say at all.' His mouth hovered over hers, whispering against her lips like an erotic promise. 'You need to start making it up to me. And this is how we are going to do it.'

With a rough movement his arms drew her to him, crushing her breasts to his chest as they wrapped around her. His lips claimed hers in a collision of fire and hunger and fierce possession, as if intending to blot out all the turmoil and confusion of the past and make this one surreal moment the only thing that mattered.

And as Leah closed her eyes, let herself go, felt herself surrender to the power and the bliss of his kiss, she found herself responding in kind. Because there really was nothing else she could do.

CHAPTER EIGHT

THROUGH THE FOG of a deeply sated sleep Leah heard familiar muffled grunts coming from the baby monitor. She stirred, her body twisting inside the tight embrace of tangled limbs, and as she opened her eyes she suddenly remembered where she was. In Jaco's bed. In Jaco's arms. With her face pressed so tightly against his neck that she could see nothing but the pink blur of his skin.

She blinked, feeling her eyelashes brush against him, inhaling his warm scent. Lifting her head, she squirmed until she had enough space to look up. And straight into the dark oblivion of Jaco's remarkable eyes.

'*Buongiorno.*' He smiled down at her, using his little finger to brush away a strand of her hair that had stuck to her lip.

'Good morning.' She elbowed herself more upright. 'How long have you been awake?'

'Awhile. But I didn't want to disturb you.

I figured that after last night you probably needed the sleep.' A wicked twinkle lit his eyes.

'I guess we both did.'

She matched his smile as the memory of the night they had spent together came rushing back in glorious Technicolor. The passion, the tenderness, the sheer erotic explosion of them coming together—it had been truly wonderful. She could still taste it on her lips, feel it in the weight of her limbs, sense the faint throb in the very core of her.

'But I suspect our son has no such compunction about waking his mother.' Gabriel's soft grunts were rapidly increasing in volume. 'I'll go and get him.'

Dropping a tender kiss onto Leah's upturned mouth, Jaco extricated his arms and legs from around her body and pushed back the tangled sheet.

'No, really.' Forcing herself back to reality, Leah stretched out a hand to his back. 'I'll go. It might confuse him if he sees you.'

'Well, the more he sees me, the less confused he will be.' Pulling on a pair of boxers, he turned and sat down on the edge of the bed. 'I mean to play an active role in my son's life. You know that, don't you?'

'Yes.' Leah nodded. 'Yes, I do.'

'Bene.' He stood up, then hesitated. 'And I'm hoping to play a pretty active role in his *mamma*'s life too.'

Bending to cup her chin in his hands, he planted another kiss squarely on her lips, then touched the tip of her nose with his finger before turning to stride out of the room.

Leah waited a couple of seconds. Gabriel's cries were now building up to full volume. Her every instinct was telling her to go to him, but Jaco was right—he did have to get to know his son. It was because of her that he hadn't been able to forge that relationship right from the start.

Through the monitor she could hear Jaco going into her bedroom. Gabriel was quiet for a moment, then came Jaco's soft words of greeting in Sicilian, the rustle as he picked him up, and a distinct gurgle of pleasure from Gabriel. Leah held herself very still, listening. She had to hand it to Jaco. Somehow—and she had no idea how he'd done it—he had already won his son's heart.

Slipping out of bed, she went into the en suite bathroom and, finding a man's towelling bathrobe on the back of the door, shrugged it on, turning back the cuffs and belting it tightly around her waist.

After rinsing her hands under the tap she

splashed water on her face, staring at her reflection in the mirror. She looked tousled and satisfied…like a woman who had just spent a wild night of passion with the sexiest man in the world. Which she supposed she had. She looked—and this was the biggest shock of all—*happy*. There was a light gleaming in her mascara-smudged eyes that had been missing for far too long.

Making her way back to her bedroom, she stopped in the doorway, grinning widely at the sight that met her eyes. Gabriel was lying on the bed, wriggling and kicking for all he was worth, while Jaco was trying to put a nappy on him.

'Come on, buddy, work with me here.'

He tried to slide the nappy under Gabriel's bottom, but Gabriel was having none of it, half rolling onto his side, squirming so that the tab fastener stuck to one chubby buttock.

'Jeez...' Jaco scratched his bed-ruffled hair. 'How hard can this be?'

'Having trouble?' Leah stepped into the room, laughing.

'Whatever makes you think that?' Jaco gave her his most innocent expression.

'Um…this.' Picking up Gabriel, Leah held him aloft and they both stared at the dangling nappy.

'Well, yeah…' Jaco frowned at his handiwork. 'Maybe there *is* room for improvement.'

'Just a bit.' Laying Gabriel down again, Leah gripped hold of his ankles and expertly repositioned the nappy. 'Why don't you go and make us some coffee while I give him a feed?'

'Buona idea.'

Jaco pulled her into a kiss before turning to leave.

When he returned a short while later, Leah was sitting up in bed with Gabriel at her breast. He paused to take in the scene, his breath catching in his throat. Gabriel had reached out to grasp a lock of Leah's hair, and was holding it in his closed fist while Leah cradled his body against hers, singing softly under her breath. For the first time he didn't feel excluded, shut out. For the first time he saw them as a family. *His family.* And he felt his heart swell with pride.

'Come on—move up.' Firmly putting a lid on the sentiment, Jaco set Leah's mug down on her bedside table, then walked around the other side of the bed to get in.

Leah looked up, surprise in her eyes, but did as she was told, shifting across to make room beside her and Gabriel.

'That's better.' Holding his mug in both hands, Jaco took a sip. 'How's he doing?' He reached across to stroke the soft dark curls of his son's hair.

'Almost done, I'd say.' As she spoke Gabriel's mouth slackened on her nipple and he wriggled in the constraints of her arms as she tried to pat him on the back to wind him.

'You want me to take him while you drink your coffee?'

'Oh, yes, please.' She passed him across, adjusting her dressing gown before reaching for her mug.

Jaco settled Gabriel in the crook of his arm and gazed down at his son. Why did this feel so right, all of a sudden? So natural? He had never given much thought to the idea of having kids except as something that might happen in the way distant future. He had certainly never envisaged himself changing nappies!

All his adult life had been spent doing deals, making money and then reaping the rewards of that success: buying luxury properties, eating in the best restaurants, dating a succession of beautiful women. He'd assumed that was the life he wanted, the life he would pick up again once he had dealt with the Garalinos. But now… Now, as he felt the

warm, solid weight of his son in his arms, and glanced across at the dishevelled sunlit beauty of the woman in bed beside him, he felt a strange sense of contentment creep over him.

And something else—something that was so unfamiliar he had to search around to put a name to it. *Happiness.* That was what it was.

Jaco realised he'd never even missed it. Since the death of his parents he had just assumed that true happiness was the prerogative of other people, or maybe it didn't even exist. His brutal upbringing at the hands of the Garalino family had certainly left no room for any sort of joy, and since then he had channelled all his efforts into making something of his life. Which he had succeeded in doing—big-time. But happiness… Nah, that was only for the very young or the very deluded.

As if to demonstrate his theory, Jaco felt the chill of a cloud pass over that chink of sunlight. The niggle at the back of his mind had fought its way forward. There was something he needed to know…

'So…' He took Gabriel's perfect little hand in his, turning it over to stare at the tiny shell-like fingernails. 'Don't take this the wrong way, but there is something I have to ask you.'

'What's that?' Leah turned to look at him, the smile in her eyes dying at the sight of his serious face.

'Other men.'

'I'm sorry?'

'Other men. Have there been any?'

'Ha!' She carefully placed her coffee mug down on the table. 'You mean in between finding out I was pregnant, going into hiding, giving birth and then being bundled off to this island, have I found time to take a couple of lovers?'

'Yes, Leah.' A muscle twitched in his jaw. 'That's exactly what I mean.'

'Then let me put your mind at rest.' With an audible huff, she folded her arms across her chest. 'The answer to your question is no.'

Grazie Dio. Just the idea of Leah in the arms of another man was enough to shake the very foundations of his control.

'What about you?'

She'd posed the question as more of a counter-attack than a quest for the truth, but the way she chewed the inside of her lip gave her away.

'No doubt there has been a veritable stream of beauties hopping in and out of your bed.'

'No.' Jaco shook his head.

'So, just one or two?'

She looked at him with such hope that Jaco felt his heart melt.

'Not even that.'

'What? No one? Really?' Incredulity mixed with wary relief danced in her eyes.

'No one, Leah.'

'Wow!' She gave him a megawatt smile.

Carefully setting Gabriel down on the bed in front of him, Jaco drew her into his arms, the need to hold her against him suddenly overpowering. Something about her vulnerability had touched him in a place he hadn't even known existed, more deeply than he had ever thought possible. And now, as they were locked in this close embrace, it occurred to him that his feelings for this woman had the potential to change his life. That so far he had allowed himself to do no more than skim the surface.

Finally they pulled apart, and Jaco leant in to kiss her again, the stirrings of desire already making their presence felt as he breathed in the delicate fragrance of her hair, her skin, the taste of her lips. The kiss started to deepen—until a loud squawk from the third party alerted them to his existence and reluctantly Jaco pulled away.

'To be continued...' He gave Leah a sinful grin before getting out of bed and scooping

Gabriel up in his arms. 'Come on, *mi figlio*, let's go and make your *mamma* some breakfast while she has a shower. If she is anything like me, she must be starving.'

Twenty minutes later Jaco surveyed his handiwork. Fruit, yoghurt, bread and jam, warm brioche rolls and a large pot of coffee, all laid on a table on the decked terrace. He had even picked a bunch of some sort of brightly coloured flowers—he had no idea what—and put them in a jug in the centre of the table.

Gabriel was propped up on an enormous beanbag in the shade, a wooden spoon in his hand, alternating between putting it in his mouth and flailing it around in an attempt to hit the upturned saucepan in front of him, his face lighting up with pleasure whenever he managed to make contact.

Jaco took in a deep breath, looking around him at the view, at his baby son, at the doorway into the living room where Leah would be appearing any minute. *He could get used to this*. More than that, he suddenly realised that this was what he *wanted*. A wife and family, kids—lots of them—so that he could give them everything he had never had. Security, happiness, *love*. For the first time ever it suddenly seemed possible.

Once this wretched business with the Garalinos was over he would be able to start his life afresh. He was so close to it now he could almost touch it, smell it. He just had to negotiate this last final push, see all his carefully laid plans through to conclusion, and his ordeal would be over. His and Francesca's. And, of course, Leah's.

Despite his macho insistence that Leah and Gabriel would be living with him whether they liked it or not, Jaco wanted Leah there of her own volition—not because he had forced her. And marriage and kids? He didn't want them with some unspecified woman in the future. He wanted them *now*—with Leah. With a starburst of clarity he realised that Leah McDonald was crucial to every aspect of his future life.

As if on cue, she appeared, her cheeks pink, her hair damp from the shower.

'Ooh.' She looked around her, bending down to retrieve the wooden spoon that Gabriel had flung to one side and giving it back to him. 'This looks lovely. And not a burnt steak in sight.'

'Less of the sarcasm, young lady.' Pulling back a chair, he gestured for her to sit with a sweep of his arm, then offered her the plate of brioche rolls. 'I'll have you know these

rolls have been removed from the freezer and oven-baked to perfection.'

'Mmm...' Leah took a bite and smiled at him. 'I won't argue with that.'

'So what do you eat for breakfast in Scotland?' He leant forward to pour her a glass of orange juice. 'Is it haggis or something?'

'Hello—stereotypical prejudices alert!' She gave him a mock-stern frown. 'I'll have you know that haggis would never be consumed until the evening meal—or high tea, as we call it.' She smeared butter onto her roll and took another large bite. 'Breakfast would most likely be porridge oats or something called a clootie dumpling. It's a bit of an acquired taste.'

'Then I look forward to acquiring it.' Jaco gazed back at her, testing the water, aware that if he wanted to gauge her feelings he was going to have to open up himself.

'Really?' Leah looked at him in surprise.

'Yes, why not? I would very much like to see your country and get to know your father. When this is all over we should pay a visit.'

'And when *will* it be over, Jaco?' Suddenly serious, Leah set down her glass and fixed him with her stunning hazel-eyed stare. 'When are you going to tell me what all this

is about? Give me back my phone? Allow me and Gabriel to leave this island?'

'Soon—I promise.' He reached for her hand. 'I wouldn't be doing this, Leah, if it wasn't vitally important.'

'So you keep saying.' She looked down at his hand, covering hers, before withdrawing her own to tuck her rapidly drying hair behind one ear. 'But I don't understand why you can't just tell me what's going on now.'

Jaco hesitated. He wanted to tell her the truth. She *deserved* to know the truth. He saw that now.

Up until last night he had seen no reason to explain anything—not after the deceitful way she had kept his son a secret from him. But now he could see that she had had her reasons. They were all wrong, of course, but in Leah's typical hot-headed, act-first-and-think-later way she had made a snap judgement and taken herself off without waiting for any sort of explanation. She was as impulsive as she was passionate, but Jaco could never hate her for that. Far from it.

'Confidentiality is of the utmost importance.' His brow furrowed as he weighed up how to proceed. 'In my experience, the fewer people you trust, the less likely you are to be let down.'

Jaco had found that out to his cost. As a naive eleven-year-old he had put his trust in the Garalino family. Worse than that, he had been prepared to love them.

Excited at being adopted into a large, powerful family of brothers and uncles, led by the charismatic Luigi Garalino, he had tried to do everything he could to please them at first, in the hope that they would show him and his little brother some of the love that had been so badly missing from their lives ever since their parents had died.

But he had soon discovered there was no love to be had from that family. And as the years had gone by it had become more and more apparent just how rotten to the core the whole lot of them were.

Years of being beaten for the slightest excuse—leaving a smear on the windscreen of the fancy limousine he had just washed, or being late back, breathless and panicking, from the errand he had run across the other side of town. Years of being denied food if he dared to answer back or tried to protect his brother. Years of being locked in the coal hole for days at a time, then beaten again when he was finally let out.

But that was nothing compared to the psychological abuse that Francesco had suffered.

The pain of his beatings was nothing to the agony of seeing his little brother cowering in a corner, shaking, his clothes soiled, unable to speak, unable to move, his spirit totally broken by the Garalinos' wicked cruelty.

The guilt of not being able to protect his sibling had lived with Jaco all his life—coloured his existence, driven him on. But at least Francesca was safe now, and very soon she would be free. And by bringing Leah and Gabriel here he had protected them too—he had done the right thing. Even though Leah most definitely didn't see it like that.

'So you are saying you don't trust me? Is that it?'

Jaco watched as Leah traced a crumb around her plate before picking it up on her finger.

'I'm saying that now, more than ever, I can't afford to make any mistakes, or for anything to go wrong. So the fewer people who know, the better.'

Leah's lips twitched slightly as she assimilated this information, suggesting she was far from happy with his explanation.

She raised her eyes to meet his. 'And is it really worth it? All this plotting and subterfuge just for some business deal?'

'This is no business deal, Leah.' Jaco held

her questioning gaze. 'It is far more important than that.' He hesitated again. 'You have to understand that I am keeping you here for your own protection—yours *and* Gabriel's. It is absolutely vital that no one knows where you are.'

Leah's hands dropped down by her sides, a flush suddenly spreading over her cheeks.

'Leah?'

'Well, actually… I meant to say…' She fidgeted in her seat.

'To say what?'

'Somebody *does* know.'

'What?' The cup in Jaco's hand clattered down onto its saucer.

'Last night, when you were in the kitchen, I phoned the police.' Leah's face crumpled apologetically.

'You did *what*?'

Kicking back his chair, Jaco reared up, towering over her with thundering fury. With his body blocking out the sun it felt as if the whole world was coming to an end. Even Gabriel stopped banging his saucepan and went completely quiet.

Leah stared up at Jaco in panic. At the corded veins in his arms from the fists that were bunched like steel. At the tendons stand-

ing out in his neck…the fierce set of his jaw, the fury in his eyes.

Even though she wasn't entirely sure her call had had any effect, she had fully intended to tell Jaco about it. Wrapped in his arms last night she had roused him to try and make her confession. But somehow other events had taken over, and in the morning, when there had still been no sign of anyone coming to 'rescue' them, she had put it from her mind.

Never had she imagined that he would react like this.

'Please tell me you are joking.' He reached down to put his hand on her shoulder. 'Tell me you haven't really done this.'

'I'm afraid I have.' Leah bit down on her lip. 'I'm sorry, Jaco, but I found your phone on the floor and rang the emergency number. But they didn't seem to believe me anyway.' She clutched at this glimmer of hope, trying to calm his madness. 'And nobody came so it must be okay…right?'

'What did you tell them?' His voice was a muted roar.

'I… I said that we were being held prisoner on this island…me and Gabriel. That we wanted to be rescued.' Her unease spread, the more she thought about it.

'*Dio*, Leah.' He ground down on his jaw. 'Did you give them my name?'

'Well, yes, but—'

'What else? What else did you tell them?'

'Nothing else.' Leah screwed up her face, trying to remember. 'I may have mentioned that you were part of the Garalino family. But I didn't have time to say anything much. You came back into the room and…'

'You mentioned the Garalinos?'

'Yes.' Leah nodded guiltily. 'I'm pretty sure I did.'

'That's it. We are leaving.'

Sweeping past her, Jaco picked up a startled Gabriel and tucked him under his arm.

'Right now. Get your stuff.'

'What? Why?'

Leaping to her feet, she rushed after him, following the two of them down the corridor to her room.

'I mean, they don't even know where we are—not really. I couldn't give them the name of the island because I don't even know it.'

'They can track my phone, Leah.' He could barely contain his rage. 'They will know where we are.'

'Well, no one has turned up yet.' Still she persevered. 'Like I said, they've probably forgotten all about it. Treated it as a prank call.'

'Pack your things.'

Flinging open the wardrobe door, Jaco pulled out her suitcase and threw it onto the bed with one hand, Gabriel still held in the crook of his arm.

He glared at her, his eyes slits of fire. 'And hurry up about it.'

Working on autopilot, Leah had started to stuff their belongings into the case when suddenly she stopped. This was ridiculous. What was she *doing*? She had already been forced to pack up and leave her home once, with no more than a minute's notice, and now Jaco was doing it again. Ordering her around, giving her no explanation, expecting her to obey his every command. Well, she had had enough.

Firmly planting her feet on the floor, she folded her arms across her chest and glared at him.

'No, Jaco. You can't keep doing this to me. I'm sorry if I have done something wrong… got you into trouble…but I am *not* the one to blame here. If you had told me in the first place what was going on I would never have had to call the police and whatever all *this* is…' she gestured at the clothes strewn over the bed '…would never have had to happen.

You need to tell me *right now* what this is all about, or I flatly refuse to leave.'

'Trust me—you are leaving. We all are.' Laying Gabriel down on the bed, Jaco closed the lid of the suitcase, snapping the clasps shut. 'Your foolish action has compromised your safety, and more importantly Gabriel's safety. We have to leave the island immediately.'

'Compromised our safety?' Leah stood her ground, even though her knees were shaking and her whole body was trembling with the shock of Jaco's violent reaction. 'Are you *sure* that's what I've done? Or have I simply blown your cover?'

With a sickening wave of dread, Leah suddenly realised she had hit upon the truth. These people who they had to be protected from weren't the bad guys. *He was the bad guy.* Jaco Valentino—suave, sophisticated billionaire businessman, with his easy charm and his impeccable manners. The man who had so easily stolen her heart. The man she had fallen in love with so deeply, so desperately, that she would never, ever recover, was nothing more than a filthy rotten criminal.

Her mind started to fly in all directions. Was that why Jaco had to keep her and Gabriel hidden away? Because they might leave

a trail for the police? Or maybe, without realising it, she had some information they could use against him. *Capezzana.* What if the vineyard was nothing but a front—some sort of money laundering operation that she had unwittingly been a part of?

And then there was Francesca. Someone else Jaco had hidden away. What was it that he had said? There were *'people who would like to hurt her'. Who* would want to hurt her? And why? Presumably the same people who posed a threat to herself and Gabriel? Were these the sort of people Jaco did business with? Violent criminals? Gangsters? The mafia? No wonder he was estranged from his adopted family. They were probably disgusted by the villainous path he had taken.

With her fervid imagination rushing to slot the pieces of the jigsaw into place, Leah saw a very ugly picture taking shape.

'You have no idea what you are talking about.'

Slashing through her thoughts with blade-like ferocity, Jaco picked up the suitcase and watched with mounting impatience as Leah stuffed the last few things into her shoulder bag, then gathered Gabriel into her arms.

Herding them from the room, he marched her out of the villa and towards the helicop-

ter that gleamed in the punishing sunshine. After making sure she was buckled in safely, with Gabriel on her lap, Jaco walked in front of the cockpit. But instead of getting in the other side straight away he strode towards the cliff-edge and, pulling his phone out of his pocket, hurled it into the sea with all his might.

With a surge of stomach-churning dread, Leah felt as if a part of her had drowned with that phone. The part that had clung to the hope that she had got this all wrong.

She had to go with him now. But the first chance she got she and her baby son were going to make a bid for freedom. She had no intention of being around this sickening man for any longer than was strictly necessary.

CHAPTER NINE

JACO SHUT THE door to his office, double-checking it had locked behind him. He took in a breath as he looked around at the gleaming wooden panelling and the sparkling mirrors, the dazzling spotlights, suddenly wondering why he had commissioned this flashy monstrosity. Even naming it *The Alessia*, after his mother, felt all wrong. In no way did it reflect her gentle personality.

At the time he had considered the luxury yacht just another compulsory toy for the billionaire playboy, along with the fast cars and the fancy properties all over the world. But Jaco was no longer that man.

The memory of all those years of hollow sex with women who had meant nothing to him now filled him with revulsion. He'd told himself he was having fun, that no-strings sex with a host of beautiful women was every red-blooded man's dream. Now he realised it

had all been a pointless waste of time. That the reason he had never wanted any commitment was because he had never found anyone he wanted to commit to.

Until Leah. Until the day Leah McDonald had burst into his life like a ray of autumn sunshine, bringing a glow of vitality to everything around her with her spirit and her smile and her infectious enthusiasm. He hadn't fully realised it at the time, but that day had been the turning point of his life.

Striding down the windowless carpeted corridor, Jaco focussed on what he had to do. Bringing Leah and Gabriel to the yacht had never been part of the plan, but Leah had left him no choice. By phoning the police she had seriously jeopardised the whole operation. And, worse still, put herself and Gabriel in danger.

Because Jaco didn't trust the police. He didn't trust anyone apart from the select few who had managed to prove themselves through rigorous checks and several years of loyal service. Everyone else he viewed with the deepest suspicion. That way there were no nasty surprises.

He had no idea who this person was that Leah had spoken to. But he did know that she had not only given them his name but

the name Garalino, which would have immediately set alarm bells ringing. One of the most powerful families in Sicily, the Garalinos were on intimate terms with both the *carabinieri* and the *polizia di stato*. Bribery, corruption and coercion was rife.

Even if Leah's call had triggered a legitimate response there was no saying that that couldn't be just as calamitous. Because walls had ears, and in the murky world that Jaco was dealing with here, those ears belonged to some very dangerous people indeed.

So rapidly moving Leah and Gabriel onto this yacht had been the only course of action. Keeping them safe was Jaco's main priority, closely followed by limiting any potential fallout from Leah's reckless action.

They were moored off the coast of Palermo, which meant he was close enough to get to the action when it all kicked off tonight. The yacht was secure enough, but even so Jaco had taken the precaution of appointing Cesare, his most trusted bodyguard, to watch over Leah and make sure she didn't pull any more stunts like the last one.

Even with just a skeleton crew on board he couldn't be too careful—he certainly couldn't afford any loose tongues. It was absolutely vital that no one knew about the sting to-

night, and that included Leah. He simply couldn't risk telling her—it was too dangerous. Left to her own devices, who knew what havoc she could wreak? She had enough fire to start a conflagration, and more courage than any woman he had ever met. Like a repelling magnet, all the qualities that he loved about her were the ones that were also driving him crazy.

Ushering her into one of the sumptuous suites with Gabriel held tightly against her chest hadn't been pleasant. The look of utter disgust she had given him when she had spotted Cesare positioned outside the door would have sent a chill through the devil incarnate. He could still see its image, scorched on the back of his retina. But it was a necessary precaution. And it wouldn't be for long.

The cargo ship from South America was on course to arrive this evening—exactly at the allotted time. The whole Garalino family would be slavering in their eagerness to get their hands on what they thought was the largest shipment of cocaine ever recorded. The international drug enforcement agencies, all meticulously vetted, were primed and ready to pounce at exactly the right moment. Everything was in place.

But it would only take one false move for everything to go catastrophically wrong.

Which was why Jaco was obsessively following every step as it happened. Like watching a gruesome game of chess, he followed the moves being made on a bank of computer screens in his office, receiving coded updates from the intelligence agents as the clock ticked ever closer to the conclusion.

With the whole Garalino family under surveillance, in numerous different locations, it was a massive operation. But it was Luigi Garalino who was the real prize. Head of the notorious Garalino family, he was the man behind a string of evil atrocities stretching back over several decades.

The man who had murdered Jaco's parents.

Jaco had only had this devastating piece of information confirmed relatively recently. Always deeply suspicious about how they had died—why their car had plunged over a cliff on a road they knew so well, with no other vehicle involved and no treacherous weather conditions—he had made it his mission to discover the truth. Eventually he had tracked down someone who had worked for the Garalino family at the time, and with enough

cash to loosen his tongue the whole sordid story had come out.

It was just as he had thought. The day Luigi Garalino's evil gaze had fallen upon the profitable Capezzana vineyard his parents' fate had been sealed. By standing up to Garalino and his band of thugs, refusing to have any part in his corrupt plans for their precious vineyard, they had had their lives snuffed out—just like that—when the brake lines on their vehicle had been cut.

Having this heinous act confirmed had consumed Jaco with a fury that knew no bounds. He had decided there and then that he would have his revenge. That he wouldn't rest until he did. And so the many months of meticulous planning had started.

Luigi Garalino thought he was invincible. That his power was so great, his evil influence so all-pervading, that no one would ever dare try to bring him to justice. Well, Jaco had news for him.

He was going to be there on the docks when that container was opened… When Garalino's most trusted henchman—a meticulously trained undercover cop—slit open a couple of specially prepared sample sacks to verify their contents. He was going to be there when the money changed hands, and he

was going to step out of the shadows at the precise moment that Garalino was arrested. When he knew the game was up. And Jaco was going to look him in the eye and swear vengeance for the death of his parents.

Leah marched up and down through the lounge area to the bedroom and then back, her steps muffled, silenced by the thick cream carpet. In a cosy cocoon in the middle of the enormous bed Gabriel slept soundly, blissfully unaware of his captivity and the truly villainous man his father was.

Jaco bringing them here and putting a bodyguard outside their door—the same brute who had evicted her from her flat, no less—had been the final straw. His explanation that Cesare was there to protect them was as patently bogus as everything else about him. Cesare wasn't there to protect them, he was there to detain them, to make sure they didn't escape—as Leah had rapidly discovered when she had tried to explain to him that his boss was an evil man, and that Cesare needed to help them to get away.

Clearly wanting to engage as little as possible with this crazy Scottish woman, Cesare had explained to her in broken English that his job was to watch over her and the child.

That was all. She'd figured that much out for herself.

Striding over to the wall of windows, Leah peered out. All around her in every direction all she could see was sea. Crossing the room, she did the same on the other side. More sea, and low sunlight sparkling on the water. There were a few boats visible in the distance. Maybe if one came close enough she could signal to them—wave a sheet out of the window or something. But closer inspection revealed that the windows were security-locked.

She could try screaming. God only knew she felt like it. She wanted to scream and shout and bash her fists against the door and the walls and the windows. She wanted to kick and fight and holler and yell until someone—anyone—came to her rescue. But what would be the point? No doubt Cesare had been instructed to restrain her if she kicked off, and even if some of the crew on board *did* hear her they would be Jaco's employees, obeying Jaco's orders.

So she was stuck—powerless, trapped. Totally at the mercy of Jaco Valentino.

Sinking down onto the sofa she picked up a cushion and buried her face in it, hot tears starting to stream down her face. Tears of

fury and frustration, but most of all tears of sorrow—for the man she had thought she had known and for the man she still loved with all her heart.

Muffled against the cushion, she didn't hear the door open or the sound of Jaco approaching. So when he reached out to touch her shoulder she let out a panicked scream.

'Per Dio!' Roughly sitting down beside her, Jaco removed the cushion from her clawlike grasp. 'Calm down, Leah.'

'Don't you *dare* tell me to calm down.' Leah scooted across the sofa to try and get away from him, all the fire and fury back with a vengeance. 'Don't you *dare* tell me how to behave. You can hold me prisoner, impose your will upon me by physically moving me from one place of captivity to the next, but you will never, *ever* tell me how to think.'

'You've been crying.' Ignoring her outburst, Jaco reached out to touch her face.

Moving away from his hand, Leah furiously brushed at her cheeks with the back of her hand. If she didn't know better, she might have thought he looked genuinely concerned.

'You really mustn't upset yourself, you know.'

'Didn't I just tell you not to tell me how to think?' She glared wildly at him.

'Oh, Leah.' He gave an exasperated sigh. '*Vieni qui*...come here.'

'No, I won't.'

But it was too late. He was already there, enclosing her in his strong arms, in the warm, drugging, mind-numbing spell of his embrace.

'Get off me.' She muttered the words against the wall of his chest.

'No.' He tightened his hold, his breath hot against the top of her head. 'Not until you've heard what I have to say.'

'I'm not interested, Jaco.' She squirmed inside his hold. 'I don't want to hear any more of your lies.'

'I have never lied to you, Leah.' Releasing the band of his arms, he cupped her face in his hands, tipping her head to meet his iron gaze. 'You can accuse me of many things, but lying is not one of them.'

'You are right—I *can* accuse you of many things. I would barely know where to start. Because lying takes many forms, Jaco, and you lie by omission.' She gave him a withering stare. 'Which is just as bad.'

'Even if that omission is for the greater good?'

'The *greater good*?' She laughed in his face. 'Who the hell do you think you are,

Jaco Valentino? Some sort of higher being who doesn't have to obey the rules of common decency? Who thinks that us lesser mortals should just mutely accept that you have all the power? Because let me tell you right now—that is never going to happen.'

'Well, for your own protection, then.' Dark brows pulled into a menacing line. 'Can you not see that there are circumstances when knowing information can be more harmful than *not* knowing it?'

'No. All I can see is a man so egotistical, so consumed with greed and power, that he no longer knows right from wrong. A man totally without morals, whose dark secrets no longer define his actions but make up who he is. Rotten to the core.'

'Is that so?' Jaco's voice was terrifyingly low.

'Yes!' Leah fired back.

'And that is your opinion of me?'

'Yes. And you know what? I feel sorry for you.'

'Really? Why would you feel sorry for such a creature?'

'Because you will end up abandoned and alone. For all the money you have made, all the fancy houses and luxury yachts you have bought…' she gestured around her '…for all

the glamorous women you have taken to your bed, you will still end up alone. Because no decent person will want anything to do with you.'

'Have you quite finished?'

'Yes…no, I haven't, actually.' She dragged in another breath. 'You need to realise that you can't treat people the way you have treated me and Gabriel and expect us to hang around. You need to take a long, hard look at yourself through the eyes of people who know you. Then perhaps you might see the person you really are, and why you lead such a solitary existence.' She fixed him with a withering stare. 'Why even your family have abandoned you.'

'Chiedo scusa?' Jaco leant forward, a sweeping dark intensity holding him terrifyingly still. 'What did you just say?'

'Well, it's true, isn't it?' Like a spark igniting the dry Scottish heath, Leah felt the fire sweep over her, taking hold. 'You have said yourself that you have no contact with your family. And just why do you suppose that is?'

'My relationship with the Garalino family is absolutely none of your business.' Pure rage emanated from every syllable. 'And I would strongly advise you to keep your misguided views on that subject to yourself.'

'What's the matter, Jaco? Touched a nerve, have I?'

'I'm warning you, Leah.'

'*Warning* me?' She leapt to her feet, throwing her hair over her shoulder. 'Just listen to yourself, Jaco. I'm not one of your mindless thugs that you can order around—who will do your bidding without question. Do you *really* think you can silence me with threats?'

'Maybe not with threats.'

Beside her in an instant, Jaco towered over her, his forbidding presence taking away her breath, eating up her air.

'But I can think of other ways.'

His mouth came crushing down on hers, hot and fierce and punishing, taking and giving in equal measure, but all on his terms. It was a kiss of purely carnal intent, to show her who was in charge, who called the shots.

And when his arms moved around her Leah responded. Because she refused to be the passive female, to try and pretend she wasn't attracted to him physically—because, frankly, they were way past that. No, she would respond in kind, give as good as she got. She would show Jaco Valentino that this fire that burned between them wasn't one-sided. That he was every bit as defenceless as she was

when it came to the raw animal passion they aroused in one another.

Linking her arms around his neck, she pulled him down, closer to her, pressing her body against his until she felt him respond. That physical, all-male response that sent such a thrill through her, liquefying her bones, melting her core. But, more importantly, she knew it was a response that he couldn't control.

Now who was in charge?

Leah opened her eyes. She wanted to see the effect she had on him as well as feel it—she wanted to live it this one last time.

Jaco altered his stance, widening his legs, and she turned her body to accommodate him, pressing herself firmly against his groin, fitting herself perfectly to him. He moaned, deep and low in his throat, and the sound resonated through her like a wave of hunger. She had caught him in her trap. Or maybe he had caught her. Either way, she was going to prove to him the power she had over him. So that when she was no longer around—and she planned to escape the first chance she got—the memory of what he was missing would continue to haunt him.

Jaco was moving her backwards now, his hands travelling down her back to her

bottom, his breathing heavy. There was no doubting where this would lead if Leah didn't put a stop to it. With superhuman effort she stiffened her body, bracing herself to push against the hot wall of muscle and sinew and skin.

Immediately she felt Jaco hesitate, giving her the space to breathe. She took it, and his arms fell away from her, dropping like weights to his sides. She stepped aside.

They stared at each other, the breath still pounding in their chests, their eyes wild with arousal. Leah swallowed, dragging her hand through her hair to push it away from her face. And then she lifted her chin slowly, deliberately, maintaining eye contact so that he could see that she refused to be the victim any more.

Jaco finally pulled his gaze away, turning to stride over to the windows before swinging back to face her again. 'It seems that we are destined to drive each other crazy.' He slanted her a wild look.

Leah remained silent, folding her arms across her chest, pursing together lips that were still throbbing from the pressure of the kiss. It was a victory of sorts. As near as she was going to get, anyway.

He advanced towards her again, but stopped

a respectful distance away. 'We can't carry on like this, Leah.'

'So you finally recognise that?' It was the first concession Jaco had ever made and Leah clung to it like a lifeline. Whatever else, she must not weaken now. She must not let this glimpse of a more vulnerable Jaco wear her down.

Neither must she let those mesmerising brown eyes that were focussed so unblinkingly on her now, nor the dark tousled curls, nor that achingly handsome face, pierce the thin protective film that she had wrapped around herself.

'Give me my freedom and we won't have to.' She concentrated on keeping her voice neutral, refusing to acknowledge the thudding of her heart.

Jaco hesitated, his face a granite mask. 'Your freedom? That's all you want?'

'Yes, Jaco! That's all I have ever wanted.'

'Then you shall have it.' He forced his hands into the pockets of his trousers. 'Very soon.'

'And Gabriel too?' A sudden terrifying thought occurred to her—that Jaco meant to separate her from her son.

'Of course.' He gave her a scathing glance. 'Though obviously I will need to have regular access to Gabriel.'

'And what does *that* mean?' She didn't trust anything he said.

'I don't know.' Exasperated, he raked a hand through his hair. 'These are all things that will need to be worked out. But I have no intention of being unreasonable.'

'Really? Well, there's a first.'

Jaco growled, the granite mask slipping to reveal his silent anger before he pulled it back into place.

He walked towards her, stopping just short of Leah's tautly held body. 'We have to find a way through this—both of us. Tell me truthfully, Leah.' His eyes delved into her soul. 'What *exactly* is it that you want?'

'Well, that's easy.' With a derisive huff, Leah willed herself to stay strong. 'I want to get as far away from you as possible.'

'Really? You are quite sure?'

He studied her face with such frightening intensity that the ground seemed to shift beneath her feet.

'Because I am not going to ask you again.'

'Yes, quite sure.' Leah backed away, swallowing to ease the tightness in her throat. 'What does it take to get through that mountainous ego of yours and make you see that I want nothing more to do with you, Jaco? Not now—not ever.'

A silence fell between them, tightening like a tourniquet.

'Very well.' When Jaco finally spoke his voice held no emotion, but the haunted look in his eyes stripped her bare. 'If that's what you want, then I will respect your wishes. As of tomorrow you will be free to leave, to go wherever you want. Other than maintaining contact with regard to my son, we need have nothing more to do with one another.'

'Well, good.' Leah fought to make her vocal cords work, to inject some conviction into her voice. 'About time.'

'I am setting you free, Leah. Not just from the necessary confinement of the last couple of weeks, but from me. From whatever it is that we have together. Or don't have. I don't know any more. All I *do* know is that it's over. This is the end. We owe each other nothing. We will go our separate ways.'

'Fine.' It was a pathetically inadequate response, but all she could squeeze out before her throat closed over completely.

'Fine.' Jaco repeated the word, but using the Italian meaning. *The end.*

He moved towards her with a silent stride, and for one heart-stopping, deliriously crazy moment Leah thought he was going to kiss her again—erase the hideously painful con-

versation they had just had with the urgent pressure of his lips, mould her against him and never let her go.

But he didn't. Capturing her eyes with a stare totally devoid of light, he slowly raised his hand, brushing the back of it against her cheek. It was a gesture so tender, so final, that Leah's heart splintered into a thousand pieces.

Then, dropping his arm, he turned and walked away.

CHAPTER TEN

THE MOTORBOAT CUT through the calm, inky water, its sound echoing in the still of the night. As he neared the yacht Jaco turned the engine off, letting the boat glide almost silently forward until he was able to jump on board and secure the ropes.

The yacht was in total darkness, with no sign of life. Climbing the ladder to the back deck, Jaco stood and looked around him, breathing the fresh, salty air into his lungs. There was a full moon tonight, casting its beam of light across the sea, owning the indigo sky.

He had done it! Tipping his head back, Jaco let the momentous realisation sink in. The sting operation had actually worked and the Garalino family had finally got what was coming to them.

Moving over to the railings, he grasped hold of the cold metal and looked out to sea.

He could hardly believe it. All the months of meticulous planning, the organisation, the investigating and the cross-checking. All the co-ordination, the manoeuvring, the deal-making, the crucial judgements he had had to make. All the necessary money that had changed hands, the danger he had put himself in. It had all paid off.

In the end it had gone like clockwork. Luigi Garalino and his two sons had walked straight into the trap and been arrested handing over a suitcase full of cash. The armed drugs squad had rounded up the Garalino henchmen and left them no choice but to drop their weapons, despite Luigi ordering them to shoot to kill.

And as Luigi Garalino had been unceremoniously bundled towards an unmarked police car Jaco had stepped out of the shadows, positioning himself in front of him and looking him straight in the eye. In the only part of the whole operation that hadn't been scripted Jaco had raised his fist and, without saying a single word, punched his adopted father square in the jaw. Because, frankly, he hadn't been able to stop himself.

Now, lifting his hand from the railings, Jaco flexed his knuckles, feeling the satisfying stiffness of the swelling. He would have

liked to do a lot more damage to that man—a whole lot more—but for now he would have to content himself with the satisfaction of a job well done.

The next stage was to prove that Luigi Garalino had murdered his parents, and he was confident he would soon have enough evidence for that. Tongues tended to loosen when long prison sentences were dangled over them—especially when 'the boss' was never going to taste freedom again.

So finally he could get his life back—whatever that life was.

Jaco's eyes focussed on the reflection of the moon on the sea, on the rippling column of light stretching towards him. He should be feeling exultant, triumphant. He should be punching the air, leaping around the deck of his luxury yacht like a man who had just conquered the world, opening bottles of champagne, seeking the company of beautiful women, staging a party to end all parties.

But the fact was Jaco didn't feel like doing any of those things. Where jubilation should have sat there was only a hollow emptiness, and the taste of victory was surprisingly bland.

He drew in a breath, then looked at his watch. It was still evening in New York. He

would make a video call to Francesca—tell her the good news. That would be sure to cheer him up.

'I can hardly believe it's all over, Jaco.'

'Trust me, it's true.' Jaco smiled back at his sister. 'I've got the injury to show for it.' He raised his knuckles to the screen to show her the swelling.

'Jaco!' Francesca gasped on a smile. 'Since when do you resort to violence? I thought using your fists was beneath you?'

'Yeah, well, there is no one further beneath me than *that* piece of scum.'

'And he really is behind bars?' Suddenly her voice was anxious again. 'I mean, there's no chance of him getting bail or something?'

'Not a chance. You don't scream "Shoot to kill!" at the police and expect to get preferential treatment. Your ordeal is over, Francesca. You can finally come out of hiding. That monster will never be able to hurt you again.'

'Oh, Jaco, thank you so, *so* much. What you have done is just incredible. Bringing that family to justice when everyone said it couldn't be done. You are officially the most wonderful man on the planet. Has anyone ever told you that?'

'Not recently, no.'

'Jaco?'

'Forget it, Fran, it's nothing.'

'No, it's not. Come on, Jaco—out with it.'

Jaco stared at the deliriously happy face of his sister, then at the image of himself in the small box at the bottom of the screen. He couldn't match that expression, nor anything like it.

He filled his lungs with air. 'Well, I've got another bit of news for you.'

'Go on.'

'How do you feel about being an auntie?'

'An auntie?' Francesca leant forward, her eyes as wide as saucers. 'Oh, my God, Jaco. You mean you are going to have a child?'

'Actually, I already have one. A son. He's three months old.'

'No!' Francesca gasped. 'But how? Why? I mean, I didn't even know you were seeing anyone.'

'I'm not.' Jaco sat back in his chair, feigning an insouciance that wouldn't fool anyone—least of all Francesca, who knew him better than most. 'At least not any more. The child is the result of a relationship I had over a year ago.'

'I see...' Francesca fixed him with her most critical stare. 'And where are they now, your son and his mother?'

'Well, they are here, actually.'

'Here? Where's "here"?'

'On board *The Alessia*. That's where I am. We're moored off the coast of Palermo.'

'So let me get this straight, Jaco Valentino.' Francesca cut straight to the chase. 'You and this woman...?' She pointedly waited for Jaco to fill in the gaps.

'Leah.'

'You and Leah and your baby son...?' She waited again.

'Gabriel.'

'You three are all cosied up together on your yacht, but you're telling me that you are not in a relationship with this Leah?'

'No, there *is* no relationship. And I never said we were cosied up—quite the reverse.'

'Meaning?'

'Meaning that she doesn't want anything to do with me.'

'So why is she there with you now?'

'Because...' Jaco sighed. 'It's a bit of a long story, but basically I needed to keep them both safe.'

'I see.' Francesca frowned deeply. 'And now?'

'Now that the Garalinos are locked up they are free to go.'

'And is that what you want?'

'It's not about what *I* want, Francesca.' Irritation scored his voice. 'I have promised Leah her freedom and now I must honour that.'

'You mean you are going to let them go? Give up without a fight? That doesn't sound like you, Jaco.'

'Maybe I'm tired of fighting. It's pretty much all we've done so far.'

'Clearly not *all* you've done.' She gave him a knowing look.

'Well, no.'

'This Leah sounds like someone who stands up for herself.'

'She is the single most infuriating woman I have ever met in my life.'

'Oh, my God!'

'What?'

'I never thought I'd see the day.'

'What?'

'You are in *love*, Jaco Valentino.' Francesca clasped her hands together in excitement.

'Nonsense.'

'Yes, you are—it's written all over your tortured face. You have to go and tell her now—right away.'

'It's the middle of the night here, Francesca.'

'So what? Off you go.' Making shooing gestures with her hands, Francesca leant for-

ward to end the call. 'Good luck. And I want to hear all about it tomorrow.'

She blew him a kiss and the screen went black.

Jaco stared at his darkened reflection. *In love?* Was it possible that Francesca was right? Would that explain why the thought of Leah leaving tomorrow felt like a blade to his heart? Why he knew it wasn't just his son he would miss so desperately, but Leah too? Would that explain the hollow feeling in the pit of his stomach and why, when he thought he had just achieved the most important goal of his life, he could take no pleasure in it?

Because finally ridding himself of the Garalino family—the leaden weight that he had dragged around with him for so long—meant that he had to say goodbye to Leah too.

Jumping to his feet, he paced around the office. The night-black windows on either side seemed to be closing in on him, making it difficult to breathe.

Leah was here, on this yacht, close by, probably curled up asleep in bed, her auburn curls spread across the pillow, her soft breath fanning the air. The image was so powerful, so visceral, that Jaco felt it rather than saw it, as if the thought of her had weakened his whole body.

He had to do something right now. Yes, it was the middle of the night, but the way he was feeling had turned time on its head—turned *him* on his head. This might be his last chance. He was going to do it. He was going tell her how he felt.

As he silently hurried along the endless carpeted corridors he tried to steady the thump of his heart. He needed to control himself. Storming in there, startling Leah and waking up Gabriel, was not the sensible way to proceed, no matter how much he wanted to do just that—to sweep her up into his arms, silence her protests with a kiss and show her what she meant to him in the way he knew best.

Now was the time for words, not actions. Long overdue words that he had kept locked in his heart for far too long. Words that he could only ever say to this one woman. To Leah.

Arriving outside her suite, he was surprised to find that Cesare was no longer there, standing guard. Alarm immediately flooded through him. Flinging open the door, he marched into the lounge, his eyes darting around as he looked for clues, his breath rasping in the silence. The bedroom door was closed but he stormed in, no longer caring

about startling them, not caring about anything other than finding Leah and Gabriel safe.

With a sickening sense of foreboding he flicked on the lights. The bed was empty. The room was empty. Leah and Gabriel had gone.

Leah stood on the upper deck, hugging Gabriel to her chest to try and keep him warm. A breeze was coming off the sea, ruffling the curls on the top of his head. But he was still sound asleep and perfectly safe.

Leah, however, felt far from safe. Her initial fury that Jaco had incarcerated them on this boat had swiftly turned to fear, the longer she was here—and the more she saw.

Refusing to stay imprisoned in her suite, she had announced to her bodyguard that she was going up onto the deck to get some air. If she had thought he would let her go alone, she had been very much mistaken. Nodding his assent, Cesare had simply followed behind them, so close that his massive body felt like an impenetrable wall. She was never going to get away from this man.

Leah glared at him now, positioned a few feet away, his arms firmly folded across his chest, his cold eyes following her every move.

She turned to look at the sea. The moon-

light was moving across the water, its eerie illumination only making her feel more isolated, more desperate. There was no escape from this floating prison.

The idea that she might have been able to sweet-talk Cesare into letting them go—maybe even taking them to the shore in a launch boat—had died before the words could even be formed. One look at his impassive mask had made it quite clear she would get nowhere with him. He was Jaco's man.

Which meant she had no alternative but to wait it out and see if Jaco would be true to his word and let them go the next day. *Set them free.* That was what he had said.

As if that would ever be possible.

Leah knew without a shadow of doubt that she would never be free from the torment of Jaco Valentino. His hold over her went far too deep—was far too ingrained for her ever to be free of him. He was a stain that could never be removed from her heart.

She started to pace the deck, walking round the circular swimming pool, its underwater lights the only illumination apart from the moon in the sky. From the railings, Cesare watched her every move, ready to pounce if she looked as if she was going to make a dash for it or try to fling herself over the side.

Mind whirring, Leah's fractured thoughts went back to what she had witnessed about an hour ago.

A fast-moving vessel, heading straight for the yacht had caught her eye. The engine had been cut some distance away, so that it had silently glided towards the back of the yacht. Jaco—it had had to be. Something that had been reluctantly confirmed by Cesare's grunt when she had put it to him.

Where the hell had he been at that time of night? The thought of him boarding the yacht under cover of darkness had only reinforced everything Leah had suspected about him. No doubt he had been meeting his 'business associates'—this was probably the kind of hour he liked to do his deals. No doubt he had been involved in something bad.

Suddenly Leah felt overwhelmingly tired, feeling the weight of everything pressing down on her, weakening her bones. She moved over to the row of padded sun loungers alongside the swimming pool and, adjusting one to the most comfortable position, settled herself and Gabriel down to wait until sunrise.

She didn't want to miss it. She didn't intend to be here a moment longer than she had to.

As soon as day broke she was going to find Jaco and demand that he honour his agreement and let them go.

Grazie Dio. Coming up onto the front deck, Jaco spotted them immediately—Leah and Gabriel, the two most precious wonders in his life. The blood pumped though his veins in a hot surge of relief.

Lying on a sun lounger, watched over by Cesare, they both seemed to be fast asleep, Gabriel pressed against his mother's chest in a sling. Why Leah had chosen to come out here rather than stay in the luxurious comfort of her room he had no idea. But they were safe. That was all that mattered.

Signalling to Cesare, who retreated into the shadows, Jaco moved towards them, stopping a few paces away. He stared down, drinking them in, finally giving himself permission to set his emotions free.

But still the power of his feelings took him by surprise. Nothing could have prepared him for the sheer rush, the swell, the deluge that hit him once the gates were opened. There was simply no containing the flood of love he felt for them both.

His feelings for his son had hit him hard and fast—like a blow to the chest. Ever since

that day on the island when he had picked Gabriel out of his crib, first held him in his arms, he had recognised that this was a very special bond, that his love for his son would know no bounds. He knew it would be with him for ever, no matter what the future might hold for either of them.

But his love for Leah… That was different altogether. So much more complex, so maddeningly unfathomable, it had taken longer to show itself, to come to the surface, simply because it had been buried so deep. But it was that same depth that now made it so unshakable, so undeniably real, rooted as it was in the bedrock of his soul. The question was, could Leah ever feel the same way about him?

Squatting down beside them, he laid a hand on Leah's arm.

Her eyes flew open. 'Get away from me!' On her feet in a second, she backed away from him, her arms wrapped protectively around Gabriel, who had started to stir. 'I don't want you anywhere near me.'

'Per l'amor di Dio.'

Jaco tried to close the gap between them, but when Leah took several more steps backwards he halted.

'Leah, stop this. You are overreacting.' He

fought to make himself sound reasonable, when all he wanted to do was take away her insulting behaviour with a blazing kiss.

'Overreacting, am I?' she demanded in the dark. 'I don't think so.'

'Yes, *you are*. There is absolutely no need for you to behave like this.'

'No? So I have no reason to mistrust you?' Leah arched her back, the wind picking up her hair and lifting it around her head.

'None whatsoever.'

'Then perhaps you would like to tell me where you have been tonight. What have you been up to?' Her eyes flashed in the dark.

Jaco stilled.

'Yes, that's right, I saw you.' Triumphant now, Leah pursed her lips. 'I saw you sneaking back in the middle of the night.'

'I can assure you, I was not *sneaking*.' A tide of frustration surged through him, and before he knew it his feet had taken him towards her, his protective hands placed solidly on her shoulders.

'Get off me!'

'No, I won't.' He wrapped his arms around her, trying his best not to squash Gabriel. 'We are going to go inside now, and then I will tell you exactly what I've been doing.'

'So that you can imprison me again, you

mean?' She raised her hands to try and push him away.

'Not this time. All I ask is that you hear my explanation. Then you will be free to go. You have my word.'

He felt her hesitate against his body.

'And why should I believe you?'

'Because it's the truth, Leah.' He loosened his hold a fraction. 'And because once you hear what I have to say everything will become clear.'

'So, tell me now.' Determination glowed in her eyes as she threw back her head to look at him. 'You can say whatever it is you have to say out here. Right now.'

Jaco hesitated. 'Very well.' He pulled in a breath, dropping his arms but taking hold of her hands until Leah gave them an aggressive shake to get them free. 'But it is getting cold. Gabriel should go back inside.'

He signalled to Cesare, who silently stepped forward.

'Cesare, would you take my son back down to Ms McDonald's suite and wait for us there?'

Displaying only the merest flicker of surprise, Cesare held out his arms obediently.

'No.' Leah stood firm. 'I'm not giving Gabriel to *him*.' She reached down to take hold

of one of Gabriel's legs that was dangling outside the sling, cupping his foot for comfort, squeezing it in her hand.

'Yes, you are. Cesare is the father of six. He is more than capable of watching over Gabriel while I talk to you.'

Leah hesitated, feeling the chill of the night breeze blowing over her face. Regarding Cesare with deep suspicion, she nevertheless released the sling from behind her back and reluctantly handed Gabriel over.

'But this is just for five minutes. And if you so much as harm a hair on his head…'

'There is no fear of that, Leah.' Jaco stated sternly. 'Protecting my son is what this has been all about.'

With Gabriel nestled in the crook of his arm, Cesare turned to take him below deck.

Tucking her windswept hair behind her ears, Leah positioned herself in front of Jaco, fire in her eyes.

'So come on, then—I'm waiting. What is this explanation that's going to change everything?'

Jaco took a step closer, holding her shining defiant gaze, physically having to stop himself from gathering her in his arms.

'*Va bene.* The reason I have had to keep you and Gabriel hidden away is because I

have been involved in an extremely dangerous and complex mission.'

'A *mission*?' Leah scoffed. 'Is that what you call it?'

Jaco ground down hard on his jaw. 'But, as of tonight, I am pleased to say it is all over. The mission has been successfully completed.'

Leah's silence simmered between them. 'And I see you have the injuries to prove it.'

Jaco followed her disgusted gaze to the knuckles of his hand, the swelling clearly visible in the light of the moon. He tucked his hand into his underarm.

'The important thing is that the plan worked and the family have been caught red-handed...'

'The family? What family?'

'The Garalino family.'

'*Your* family?'

'They are not *my* family.' Jaco swallowed an embittered breath. 'Luigi Garalino is a sadistic, evil bastard.' He paused for a moment to steady himself. 'But now, finally, I have managed to remove him from my life for ever.'

'What...? You mean...?'

'*Dio*, Leah!'

Jaco caught the look of horror on her face and it struck him like a boot to the chest.

What sort of person did she think he was? What the hell did she think he was capable of doing?

He raked a hand through his hair, forcing himself to calm down, to get back on track. 'What I mean is…' he spoke slowly and clearly '…that Garalino and his sons and all their accomplices have been arrested by the police. And they will be put away for a very long time.'

'Oh…' Her mouth fell open in a deliciously soft pout. 'I had no idea.'

'No, nobody did. Secrecy was of the utmost importance.'

'I see.'

Leah turned her head away, her profile lit by the moon; her nose and upper lip, her chin, the sweep of her neck, highlighted as if by the tip of a silver pen. She was so beautiful. Suddenly all the irritation and frustration, the sheer, crazy exasperation of everything that was Leah McDonald fell away, until Jaco was left with nothing but the pure, distilled truth.

He loved her. It was as simple as that.

But it was not a truth he had shared with her.

'So that means Gabriel and I are now free to go?'

Somewhere in the fug of his addled brain

he realised that Leah was still talking, speaking her words into the void of the night, as if she couldn't bring herself to look at him. She was talking about leaving. He had to explain—quickly. He had to make her see what was in his heart.

'No!' Alarm clawed at him, and without thinking he made a grab for her hand again.

'I knew it!' Leah snatched it back, facing him full-on again. 'I *knew* you didn't mean it. I knew I couldn't trust anything you say.'

'Leah, listen to me!'

'What? So you can try and talk me round? Not a chance.' She turned roughly away from him.

'At least let me explain.' He reached for her arm to try and turn her back, but she sidestepped him. 'I'm not saying you *can't* leave…' He dragged some air into his lungs. 'I'm saying I don't *want* you to leave.'

Leah swung back in surprise. 'Why? Why would you possibly want me to stay?'

'Because…'

'It doesn't matter.' Like a gathering storm, Leah swept on. 'One way or another, Gabriel and I are getting off this boat as soon as we possibly can—and that's all there is to it.'

'No!' He reached out to her again. Leah batted at his hands until he caught them, hold-

ing them against his chest. 'Not until you have heard what I have to say.'

'Nothing you could say to me would make any difference.' She shoved against him, pushing him away, losing her balance so that she stumbled backwards towards the edge of the pool.

'*Dio*, Leah—be careful.'

Instinctively Jaco caught her in his arms to steady her, his heart thumping.

He exhaled slowly to try and calm things down. 'You might not want to hear it, but I'm going to say it anyway. The fact is…'

He kept his hands weighted on her shoulders to hold her steady, feeling her muscles and bones shift beneath his hold, sensing the fragility of her, how very precious she was. All that passion and heat and fire in such a delicate, slender frame. It was now or never.

'The fact is… I love you, Leah McDonald.'

There was a shocked silence. For a second Leah went completely still, but then with a burst of energy she came to life again, holding her arms out in front of her so that they slammed into his chest, twisting out of his grasp so that she could see his face.

'What did you just say?'

'I love you.' He repeated the words softly into the dark.

'No!' She gazed at up him. 'You can't. That can't be true.'

'Oh, but it is, Leah.'

A wary silence fell between them.

Taking a step forward, Jaco meant to close the gap between them, but with a slight shake of her head Leah backed away. His arms shot forward to try and grab her, but he was too late. There was a small gasp, followed by a resounding splash.

Leah had tumbled backwards into the pool.

CHAPTER ELEVEN

DIVING STRAIGHT IN, Jaco was beside her in a couple of seconds, scooping Leah up into his arms and wading towards the shallower water until he could safely set her down.

'What *is* it with you, Ms McDonald?' He pushed the streaming wet hair away from her face. 'Why are you so determined to drown yourself in front of me?'

'I'm not!' Leah spluttered on a watery cough, rubbing her eyes and blinking furiously. 'At least, not intentionally.' She picked up a clump of hair and lifted it over her shoulder. 'But thank you anyway. For the rescue, I mean.' She looked up at him almost shyly.

'*Prego*. You're welcome.' Jaco wrapped his arms around her, holding her close. 'If rescuing you became my life's work I would do it gladly. I would never let any harm come to you. You do know that, don't you?'

'Yes.' She trembled against his neck, her words muffled. 'I think I do.'

Jaco closed his eyes, savouring the moment. They were standing in a swimming pool, waist-high in water, fully clothed and soaked to the skin, but somehow it didn't matter. Nothing mattered except this sweet moment of happiness. For several seconds they stayed like that, locked together, swaying slightly with the giddy absurdity of it all.

Finally Leah tipped back her head, searching Jaco's eyes for clues. 'What you said before…'

She sounded so unsure, so vulnerable, that Jaco felt his throat work on a painful swallow.

'It's true, *mia cara*.' He rushed to take away her doubt, cupping her face in his hands, gazing down at her. '*Ti amo*. I love you, Leah.'

'You *love* me?' She repeated the words as if in a sort of daze, and her eyes, fringed by clumps of dark lashes, widened as she stared at him.

'*Sí*, I do. More than I ever thought possible…more than anything in the world.'

'But how…? I mean why…? How can this have happened?' She pushed away slightly, her brow furrowed with confusion.

'All too easily.' Jaco pulled her back into his arms. 'I admit I have tried to fight it, and

that there have been times when you have driven me completely crazy, but when you feel something *here*, deep in your heart, there's not a thing you can do about it.'

'Really?' She angled back her head, watching him cautiously.

'Really.' He was surprised at how easy it was to say. As if by stating his declaration out loud all the barriers between them had tumbled down like dominoes.

Leah's frown cleared and she gave him a look of such happiness, such open honesty, that Jaco felt his heart soar with hope. But as he held her to him, willing her to tell him that she had feelings for him too—something, anything, to give him some hope—he felt her slender body shiver violently in his arms.

What was he doing, selfishly keeping her here like this, letting her freeze to death?

'Come on—we need to get you inside.'

Sweeping her up into his arms again, Jaco moved them to the side of the pool, negotiating the metal steps one-handed, before setting her down and firmly taking hold of her hand, leading her below deck, their feet squelching along the carpeted corridors, until they were back at Leah's suite of rooms.

Crossing the threshold, Jaco switched on the light and they gazed at one another, be-

mused, bedraggled, speechless. Water pooled at their feet.

Cesare appeared silently from the bedroom, a look of concern on his face at the sight of the two of them, until Jaco quickly assured him that everything was fine. After solemnly stating that the child was still asleep, he was thanked by Jaco and told he could go.

Jaco closed the door behind him and then turned to Leah.

Gazing at him in bewilderment, Leah searched the depths of his eyes to make sure this was actually happening. Here was the man she loved with all her heart. *And he loved her too!*

With his shirt plastered across his chest, every powerful muscle accentuated through the transparent fabric, his trousers sticking to him like a second skin, it was all she could do not to gasp at the wonder of him. Was it really possible that he could love her anything like as much as she loved him?

Somewhere inside her doubt started to fray the edges of her happiness.

Leaning forward, Jaco traced her jawline with fingers that had a slight tremble, and through the fog of her mind Leah could hear him telling her that they had to get out of their wet clothes. He was unfastening his shirt but-

tons, tugging the wet cotton over his torso and throwing the shirt on the floor. His trousers soon went the same way.

'Your turn.'

He stood before her, wearing nothing but a pair of sodden boxers that clung to his shape, leaving little to the imagination. With his arms folded across his chest, his wet skin gleaming in the bright light, he looked simply magnificent.

'Unless you would like me to do it for you?'

Leah moved unsteadily towards him, wanting nothing more than for Jaco to strip her bare, to take her in his arms and never let her go. But despite his macho show of glorious manhood, his teasingly seductive tone, and despite the heart-melting half-smile that threatened to undo her completely, Leah could see that his eyes were wary…serious. Yes, deadly serious.

He was waiting for her to speak. Waiting for her to reveal how she felt about him.

She reached up, cupping his face, her fingertips grazing over the rasp of stubble. How could it not be patently, painfully obvious that she loved him with every fibre of her being?

To Leah it had always felt as if she wore her love for him like an uncomfortable skin—a transparent layer that meant he could see

through her to everything he meant to her. As if she gave herself away with every blush, every lowered glance, every barbed comment. But it seemed that Jaco needed proof.

Rising onto tiptoes, she pulled his beautiful face down to hers to plant the softest of kisses on his lips. Jaco groaned quietly against her mouth, his arms automatically moving over her bare back, pressing her against his chest.

Leah linked her arms around his neck, threading her fingers through his wet curls. She parted the cushion of her lips, breathing against him, sliding the tip of her tongue along the seam of his mouth until he opened it for her and she found the tip of his. He groaned again, more loudly this time, crushing her against him, and his glorious near-nakedness sent a thrill of sexual awareness to her core.

The kiss burst into flames until they were lost to it, swept along by its raging heat. But suddenly Jaco stopped, prising his lips away on a tortured breath, the hands that had roamed to her bottom stilling where they lay.

'I need to know, Leah.' He gazed at her with eyes of the darkest, deepest brown, searing into her very soul. 'I need to know if you can find it in your heart ever to love me.'

'Oh, Jaco!' The words choked out on a sob

of emotion, a solitary tear sliding down her cheek. 'Of *course* I love you. I have always loved you and I always will.'

'Grazie Dio.' Holding her eyes for a long, dazed moment. Jaco traced the path of her tear with his thumb, leaning forward to kiss her damp cheek. 'Then you truly make me the happiest man in the world.' He paused, his face darkening. 'Though I don't know what I have done to deserve your love after the way I have treated you…'

Leah touched a finger to his lips. 'We have both made mistakes. I should never have thought all those awful things about you.'

'You had every right.' He kissed her finger, then clasped her hand in his. 'I know I have to try and make amends. But first let's get you warm.'

Leading her through the bedroom, where Gabriel's sleeping breaths lightly stirred the air, Jaco went into the bathroom and turned on the taps of the large circular bath.

Leah stood motionless, still in a daze, as he started to strip off her wet clothes, obediently raising her arms so that he could pull her sweatshirt over her head, then unclip her soggy bra to release her breasts. She felt them tighten with pleasure as he pressed featherlight kisses over them.

Lifting first one leg and then the other, she let him peel off her jeans and her panties, and watched as he stayed crouched at her feet, trailing his lips up her legs, along her inner thighs, until he reached her most intimate place, making Leah stiffen in glorious anticipation.

His breath was hot against her cold skin as he laid soft kisses against her, using his tongue to make her shudder and whimper with longing. He was saying something now, something dark and sexy, spoken in his native tongue, his words partly lost in the thunder of water.

Leah had no hope of understanding what he'd said. It didn't matter. Gazing down at his bent head, blurred and out of focus beneath the rising steam, she simply let her eyes close against the bliss.

'Bath.'

Coming up to stand, he lifted her effortlessly into the bubbling water and she slid down until she was submerged up to her neck. Pulling off his boxers, Jaco settled himself beside her.

'Nice?'

'Mmm…' Leah sighed with pleasure. The heat, combined with the lack of sleep and

the rollercoaster of emotions this evening had brought, made her close her eyes again.

Jaco took hold of her hand under the water. 'There is so much I want to say to you, Leah. So much I need to explain.'

'There's no need, really.' Leah turned drowsily to face him. 'You did what you felt you had to do.'

'But I was wrong. Wrong not to tell you the truth. Not to realise you were the one person I could trust. Instead I made everything worse by holding you against your will, refusing to talk to you, behaving like a jerk. I treated you very cruelly. Can you ever forgive me?'

'I'll think about it.' Hiding a smile, Leah raised her hand to gently touch Jaco's lips, then let it drift under the water and down his chest, watching as his nipples tightened and his abs flexed beneath her touch. 'I suppose I haven't always been the easiest person to get along with.'

'True.' Jaco mirrored her covert smile. 'You've been a nightmare.' He caught her hand before it could travel any lower. 'It's hard to believe that someone so lovely could have caused me so much trouble.'

'Trouble is my middle name.' Leah gazed at him, suddenly serious. 'You should know that.'

'No, it's not, Leah. You must never think that. We've both had our fair share of problems in the past, but that's all over now. The future is what matters, and I intend to make yours as happy as I possibly can. That's if you will let me, of course.'

Leah hesitated, feeling the doubts creeping in again. Was it possible that Jaco could ever *really* make her happy? He said that he loved her now, but what if he didn't truly mean it, or if it was some sort of temporary aberration? What if she was making another stupid mistake? One from which she would never recover.

'Leah?' Jaco's eyes had darkened. 'What is it?'

'I need to be sure, Jaco.' She swallowed painfully. 'I mean totally, one hundred per cent sure.'

'*Certo*—I understand.' He stiffened, moving slightly away. 'I'm rushing you. I'm sorry. It was stupid of me to expect you to make a decision when I have just sprung this on you. Take all the time you need. I will wait as long as it takes for your answer.'

'Oh, Jaco.' Leaning in, Leah stole his words with a light kiss. 'I don't mean I need to think about my feelings for you. If anything, I love you too much. And that's the problem…'

'But why? I don't understand.'

'Because if you were to change your mind…'

'Never!'

'If you were to decide that you don't want to be with me after all and the relationship breaks down…'

'That will never happen, Leah.'

'I honestly don't think I could bear it.'

'You will never have to. *Lo prometto.* I promise.'

'I want to believe you, Jaco, really I do. But I've messed up so many times in my life I no longer trust my own judgement.'

'Then trust mine. It's *always* right.'

'Oh, Jaco.' Leah's laughter was choked with tears. 'I do love you.'

'*Bene.* Then that is all that matters.' He kissed her softly on the lips. 'Because I love you too.' He linked their fingers, squeezing tightly. 'I'm just sorry it took me so long to recognise it. I have been focussing on hate for so long that it had begun to consume me. I see that now. To the point where I barely recognised love, even when it slapped me in the face.'

'Slapped you in the face?' Leah giggled. 'Is that what happened?'

'Yes, it did.' Jaco's brow furrowed in mock

concern. 'In fact I think *you* may have tried a physical slap once or twice.'

'Hmm...' Leah pulled an apologetic face. 'Sorry about that.'

'Don't be. You have no need to be sorry about anything. I'm the one who should be apologising. I was so twisted up with hatred that I couldn't see straight.'

'Because of the Garalino family, you mean?'

Jaco nodded grimly. '*Sí.* You have no idea how evil they were, Leah.'

'Then tell me.'

Jaco hesitated, a muscle working in his jaw. 'They blighted my childhood, which was bad enough, but they almost destroyed Franc. He wasn't as strong as me—on top of which, he was struggling with his gender nonconformity issues. The Garalinos persecuted him mercilessly.'

'Oh, Jaco, I'm so sorry.'

'And do you know what tortures me more than anything else?'

Leah felt her heart constrict with pain at the sight of Jaco's anguished face.

'The fact that I put my trust in this evil family—to start with at least. That when we were children I tried to make Francesco fit in...bullied him into doing what they wanted

to try and save him from another beating. I didn't protect him as I should.'

'But you were so young, Jaco. You wouldn't have known any better.'

'I should have done more. I should have taken Franc with me when I escaped to New York.'

'I'm sure you did everything you could at the time. You must *never* blame yourself for the Garalinos' wickedness.'

Jaco shook his head despondently.

'So that explains why you have been so protective of Francesca ever since?' Leah's voice was soft.

'*Sí*, I suppose it does. But there is something else.' He hesitated again, dragging in a deep breath. 'Luigi Garalino killed my parents.'

'No!' Leah's hands flew to her mouth.

'I'm afraid it's true.' He waited for the horror to sink in before catching her hand and holding it to his mouth. 'There—now you know everything. Now you know why I have found it so hard to trust anybody ever again.'

And in that moment Leah *did* know. More than that, she knew that he really did love her. She could see it in his eyes, hear it in his voice, feel it in the way he had laid himself bare.

'Don't cry, Leah.' Jaco stroked his finger down her cheek, removing the silent tears she hadn't even known she was shedding. 'The past is over—done with. This is about the future. A future that I could never have imagined twelve months ago. You, me and Gabriel. *My family.* Who would have thought?'

The clouds parted as his handsome face cleared.

'What with all the horror and anger, the nightmare of trying to bring the Garalinos to justice, I had never given any thought to having a family of my own. And yet here you are, right before my very eyes.'

Leah felt the emotion shining from his soul, its warmth radiating through her like a sunbeam.

'And I haven't even thanked you yet.'

'I don't need thanks, Jaco.'

'Oh, but you do. Thank you, Leah. Thank you *un milione di volte* for the precious gift of our son. You have no idea what that means to me.'

Leah swallowed, biting down on her lip. She loved this man so much.

'Well…' The twinkle of tears in her eyes turned into something more mischievous. 'I didn't make him all by myself, you know.'

'True.' Jaco matched her look. 'Maybe it's time to remind ourselves just how we did it.'

'Maybe it is.'

Drawing her to him, Jaco enveloped her in his strong embrace, tangling their legs beneath the water, pressing himself seductively against her. With their bodies sealed together, Leah sighed with happiness.

'I love you, Leah McDonald.' Jaco breathed the words into her hair. *'Ti amo moltissimo.'*

As the warm steam rose around them he peeled them apart just enough to bring his lips down on hers, to kiss her with all the passion and possession of a man intent on proving just that.

With the sun beginning to rise over the sea, Jaco adjusted the throw around Leah's shoulders and glanced down at his son, who was wriggling on her lap.

'You're sure you're not cold, either of you?' He looked doubtfully at Gabriel, who gave him a broad, gummy grin in return.

'We're fine.' Leah turned to smile at him, raising her hand to smooth Gabriel's curls. 'You are talking to a girl raised in the Highlands here. And Gabriel…' She lifted him up under the arms so that she could adjust his position on her lap. 'He's just thrilled to have

anyone awake with him at this ungodly hour of the morning!'

'He certainly seems ready to start the day.' Jaco tickled his son under his chubby chin.

It had been Leah's idea to come up onto the deck to see the sunrise. Neither of them had had any sleep, unwilling to waste a single precious moment of the night.

They had settled themselves on the sofa in the lounge, talking in hushed whispers as Leah had gently probed Jaco about his past—the Garalinos, their part in his parents' deaths, his cruel upbringing—until Jaco had firmly kissed away her tears of sorrow and insisted they moved on.

So instead they had discussed the future—making plans, sharing their hopes and dreams. And they had made love slowly, tenderly, revelling in the incredible intensity of feelings they aroused in one another, stunned by the power of true love.

When Gabriel had woken for a feed about an hour ago they had torn themselves from each other's arms and slipped into bed on either side of him. Gabriel's delight at having two people to entertain him evident in the way he had shown absolutely no intention of going back to sleep. So they had thrown on some clothes and come up here into the

salty fresh air, seating themselves on one of the wide cushioned loungers, positioned for the best view of the sunrise.

Now, pressed against Leah so tightly that there was not a whisper of space between them, Jaco revelled in the warmth from her body that was seeping into his side, the sound of her soft breathing, the scent of her hair as she angled her head against his neck.

This was happiness, he realised. Pure, unadulterated happiness. And he was so full of it that he thought his chest might explode.

'Beautiful, isn't it?' Leah gazed at the fiery sky, painted so dramatically with reds and oranges, turning the water to a milky blue. 'You want to bottle it so that you can take out the cork and look at it any time you want.'

'You don't need to do that, *mia cara.* I can offer you all the sunrises you like.' Jaco reached to take Gabriel from her lap. 'And sunsets and starry nights and cloudless skies. Sicily has an abundance of such things.'

'It does, doesn't it? I love it here—you know that.'

'So it's agreed?' He gazed at her hopefully. 'We will make Sicily our home?'

'Agreed.' Leah kissed him affectionately on the cheek.

'Capezzana?'

He heard the businessman in him hurrying to close the deal. Because he knew with absolute certainty that this was the most important deal of his life. That if he didn't have Leah by his side—permanently and for ever—he would never be whole.

'Capezzana would be wonderful.'

'Grazie.' Jaco pressed a kiss to her lips, then turned his attention to his son, jiggling his knees to rock him from side to side, which produced a throaty, gurgling laugh of innocent pleasure.

Behind him, the rising sun highlighted Gabriel's curls, the halo effect making him look like a little cherub—albeit one in a stripy sleepsuit.

Never had Jaco thought himself capable of such a depth of love for a child, even his own flesh and blood. And never had he imagined an intensity of love such as he felt for Leah—so fierce, so all-consuming that it almost hurt.

'I can't wait to meet Francesca.' Leah broke through his thoughts, gazing at him lovingly. 'When are you going to introduce us?'

'Very soon, I promise.' Jaco tucked a windblown strand of hair behind her ear. 'I know the two of you are going to get along famously. In fact…' He glanced back at Ga-

briel. 'I'll be looking to you for some male support, *mio figlio.* Once those two gang up on us we won't stand a chance.'

'And don't forget Harper.' Leah gave him a playful smile. 'Gabriel hasn't even met my twin sister yet, or his little cousin, Alfie.' She paused, suddenly serious. 'Trying to keep Gabriel a secret from Harper was the hardest thing. It was inevitable that I would crack in the end.'

'And I'm very glad you did. If you hadn't told Harper, and Harper hadn't told Vieri, and Vieri hadn't told me…'

Leah cast him an apologetic glance. 'It scares me to think that if it hadn't been for that we might never have…'

'Let's not dwell on the past, *cara.*' Jaco laced his fingers through hers. 'Let's look ahead. In fact, there's something—'

'I know what we should do!'

Leah spun around to face him full-on, her eyes dancing with excitement, stopping Jaco in his tracks. He thought that he had never seen her look more beautiful.

'We should have a party. At Capezzana. We could invite everyone we know and love.'

Jaco hesitated. He had something far more important on his mind. Something that wouldn't wait a moment longer.

'We could.' He brought her hand up to his lips, lightly kissing her knuckles. 'But I have a better idea.'

'You have?'

'Sí.' He hesitated. He had to be sure he found the right words. 'Instead of a party we could have a wedding.'

'A wedding?' Her eyes brightened with shock.

'Sí.'

With her heart in her mouth, Leah watched as Jaco rose to his feet and carefully settled Gabriel on the cushions of the lounger. For a moment his tall frame blocked out the fiery ball of the sun, but then, in a dramatically graceful movement, he was down on one knee before her, one hand behind his back, the other reaching for her free hand.

'I love you. Leah, with every beat of my heart, every thought in my head. I love you far more than there are words to say it. So I am just going to ask you this…' He paused, his throat working on a swallow. 'Leah Mc-Donald, *vuoi sposarmi*? Will you marry me?'

'Oh, Jaco!' Jumping to her feet, Leah brought him up to stand with her, flinging her arms around his neck, pressing herself to him. 'The answer is *yes*.' She drew back

to look into his eyes. 'Yes, yes, a thousand times *yes*!'

Silhouetted by the sun, their bodies entwined, they sealed their pact with a lingering kiss, lost in the wonder of love.

Behind them a small person raised his chubby fists in the air, waving them about in celebration, impatiently waiting for someone to notice him. When that didn't work he tried a loud squawk, followed by a winning smile when they finally turned to look at him.

Ah, *that* was better. Swooped up by his father, he snuggled into the crook of his arm, popping his thumb into his mouth. All was well with the world.

* * * * *

If you enjoyed
Kidnapped for Her Secret Son,
you're sure to enjoy these other stories
by Andie Brock!

The Shock Cassano Baby
Bound by His Desert Diamond
The Greek's Pleasurable Revenge
Vieri's Convenient Vows

Available now!